The Gypsy Fortuneteller

Susan C. Barto

THIRD EDITION

©opyright 2003, 2008, 2013 by Susan C. Barto

Library of Congress Control Number:

2001132203

ISBN-10: 0-9712516-8-1

ISBN-13: 9780971251687

Gary Drury's Publishing™

Kentucky

Produced in The United States of America.

DEDICATION

I dedicate this book
to my precious son
William M. Barto, Phd

CONTENTS

SLUMBER PARTIES

Jean threw the first slumber party. Susannah and Jean at that time in the seventh grade belonged to a group in the process of forming. Some of the girls in this newly grouped crowd Jean had chosen and some Susannah had chosen as she and Jean had been close in grade school and wanted to remain part of the same crowd now in junior high. Therefore, at the time of the slumber party Susannah knew some of Jean's new friends only by sight. She looked forward to bonding with them and to laughing with one Elaine who according to Jean lived up to the rumors circling about her regarding her quirky sense of humor.

Jean's parents agreed to host the party with only one stipulation. No boys allowed. As most of the girls hadn't been in junior high long enough to have a particular boyfriend of the moment this edit didn't pose too large a problem. The scheduled Friday finally arrived, and Susannah felt it had been worth the wait when she saw what a glorious autumn evening it turned out to be. First all ten of them clustered in the same row of the local movie theater and watched a comedy date movie impatiently — anxious for the slumber part of the party to blast off.

Once back at Jean's, Susannah thrilled with the other girls to see the family room turned into a dormitory with ten mattresses on the floor so close together they touched each other. Apparently, Jean had extracted a promise from her parents and siblings not to enter the sacred territory as Susannah never spotted a soul other than their party members until the next morning. Jean distributed cold cokes and served chips, candy and cupcakes; and the party started.

"Jean, no boys know about tonight do they?" Susannah asked.

"Not so far as I know."

This brought forth a disappointed wail from the rest of the girls, but they soon turned to snacking and delving into the toppling pile of comic books Jean had provided. Around midnight they turned the TV on determined to stay awake through the Late and the Late Late.

"I know," the irrepressible Elaine said, "Let's pour water on the first girl who falls asleep."

As Elaine actually followed through with her threat the exhausted girls managed to keep their eyelids from drooping well Into the small hours of the morning. When dawn approached Susannah felt glad she'd survived and from the looks of the others they felt proud of themselves. This represented a milestone as Susannah knew it would not be the last slumber party.

Susannah's friend Betty threw the second slumber party, and although no boys allowed remained the rule Betty had two handsome older brothers who would be at the location by virtue of their happening to also live there. Since Susannah nursed a hopeless crush on Betty's oldest brother, Dick, she shopped for weeks choosing her bedtime attire and finally settled upon a red striped nightshirt she thought fetching. The two brothers came home and discovered the girls and their mattresses spread across the living room and sprawled into the den.

"Hi, Susannah," Dick tossed off in passing the assorted mattresses and thereby assured Susannah's happiness for the rest of the slumber party.

In the spring of that same eighth grade year Liz threw a slumber party on the night that Susannah attended the Viking Dance given by her boyfriend's HI-Y group. Susannah walked over to Liz's after Chuck dropped her off as he wasn't allowed to escort her to Liz's house which resembled a messy dormitory at that point. When Susannah arrived bubbling with news about Chuck and the dance the other girls shushed her saving,

"Not now, Sue, we're watching this prison movie."

She chalked their rudeness up to jealousy about her being the only one who had gone to the dance and settled down to the fun.

Susannah's turn to throw a slumber party occurred the following Halloween — a momentous occasion as she and her crowd decreed that it would be their last trick or trick time since they now were poised on the brink of adulthood with high school approaching next year. Susannah hoped that this party wouldn't be the last slumber party for her and her friends. Word had got around that they would be at her house after trick or treating for a slumber party. The grapevine spread the news among the boys as well as the girls. As the girls nervously trick or treated they wondered whether the boys would really show later at Susannah's house.

After they had changed into their night things they began to giggle and speculate about who would arrive and when.

"They better not come," Susannah said, "because my father said It would be the last time I could give or go to one if they do."

"Me, too," echoed one of her friends.

Betty laughed and said, "I hope they do come. Dennis has to see me in my pajamas one of these days!"

This shocked the rest of the group into silence. The silence lasted only seconds, however, because the girls heard boys' voices outside. It sounded as though they planned to storm the citadel. Some of the boys rang the bell, others knocked the knocker, and still others tapped at the windows. Susannah had just enough time to open the door to try to ask them to go away and stop the noise.

"You're going to wake the dead. Quiet!"

Her warning came too late. The boys pushed and shoved their way into the living room, and Susannah's father ran down the staircase and into the room where he promptly ordered the troop of boys out as fast as they'd entered. He allowed the girls to go on with their slumber party, but the girls knew that the entrance of the boys to the forbidden territory signaled the end of this heretofore innocent pleasure. Susannah teased Betty about the incident often asking her whether it had been worth it to have Dennis see her in her pj's.

THE NEW YEAR'S
EVE PARTY

Inviting Chuck to the party constituted the party's raison d'etre. Suellen had recently noticed a coolness on his part and thought it might be caused by her having accepted a date from her studious friend, Charlie, to go to a movie. She thought it strange that both boys with whom she was presently involved had the same name. Fortunately, Chuck responded only to Chuck and Charlie only to Charlie. It made things easier. Chuck should have realized that she felt overwhelmed by the strength of her crush on him, and she thought he knew that she and Charlie had a just friendship thing going. She'd seen Chuck and Charlie having lunch together in the cafeteria the Monday after her movie date with Charlie. She thought this to be strange as they traveled in completely different circles. Chuck in the most popular crowd, and Charlie in a slightly lower circle although he definitely didn't fall in the nerd category. Anyway, after the lunch the boys shared, Suellen's relationship with Chuck seemed kaput!

"What on earth do you think they talked about, Betty, at that lunch Whatever it could have been about ever since it happened Chuck seems cool, and Charlie is acting as though we had a romantic relationship."

"Obviously, they discussed you. But we'll never know why. Maybe one of Chuck's friends spotted you at the movies with Charlie and told him. You definitely should have cleared your date first with Chuck."

As Suellen saw the truth in Betty's final words, she felt remorse and a great desire to mend things with Chuck. Even the thought of losing his affection pricked. That's when she came up with the idea of a huge New Year's Eve party. One big enough to invite everyone including Chuck and Charlie. As they attended junior high and not high school this party would be the first New Year's Eve party their group had ever given. Chuck would be sure to come. She'd invite him first. He acted so warmly when Suellen invited him that she fell all her loving, gushy feelings return in a rush. Maybe, everything would be all right after all. Not only Chuck; but kids from at least two or three different groups accepted her invitation as well. Betty, her best friend, shared Suellen's optimism regarding her possible success in healing the rift with Chuck. Betty's black wavy hair and brown eyes looked slightly like Suellen's, and since they hung, out together so often people sometimes confused the two of them although Suellen thought that Betty possessed oodles more beauty than she did.

So far the only problem with the party's planning was Suellen's father. He and Suellen's mother generously gave permission to use their rec room for the party and to invite as many friends as she wanted. But he stipulated before the party that he wanted a printed list of all the boys attending. He actually intended to check them in as they arrived. Knowing her father's methods as well as she did, Suellen figured that he must be worrying about crashers. As if anyone would want to crash the party! And what a compliment if anyone should try. However, he

remained adamant, and Suellen resigned herself to going along with this nonsense if she wanted to have the party. Suellen dressed with extreme care making sure to put on Channel #5 as well as the new dress she'd purchased for the party. Betty arrived first so as to help Suellen bear the embarrassment of her father's standing sentinel at the front door until all the guests arrived.

"Sue, I'm so excited. Bobby's coming, and he said he couldn't wait to see me. Maybe by midnight you and Chuck will be an item again."

"That's what I'm praying for. He's still friendly to me, but friendly is the operative word. I don't want friendly. I want well you know. Isn't it strange we're both wearing little black dresses tonight, and we didn't plan it?"

Somehow Suellen managed to get through the ordeal of her father's guard duty, and soon the party was swinging along. Her parents had agreed to stay upstairs except for bringing down refreshments so she was spared further agony over her father's potential behavior. Chuck looked so handsome tonight that it was difficult to talk with him and keep her voice steady. He behaved as usual but did he seem detached or maybe she was reading more into his demeanor than the situation warranted? She'd know by midnight because she knew that just before the witching hour approached the group would form into

14

couples for the midnight kiss. Everything rolled along smoothly until the doorbell rang, and her father finally used the list and his authority. He ordered two boys from the class above hers to leave since their names didn't appear on that darn list. Popular and handsome boys too.

Finally, midnight approached. Suellen's eyes never left Chuck, and as she watched in horror he approached not her but Betty. Bobby drew in front of Betty at the same time, and to further complicate matters Charlie walked to Suellen's side with a proprietary air.

"Betty," Suellen overheard Chuck say, "Do you want to be with me at midnight?"

Suellen held her breath as Betty replied, "Thank you, Chuck, but I'm here with Bobby."

Giving Chuck one last furtive glance, Suellen turned to Charlie and tried to smile. She'd forfeited the nicest romance she'd ever had for her friendship with him, and she decided that instead of escaping to her room in tears as she wanted to do she'd accept defeat gracefully and like Scarlet ponder over it and cry tomorrow.

BOYFRIENDS

June's friends told her that she sparkled with as much sunshine as her name. June loved her name because it represented the month that contained her birth date, and she delighted in knowing that her birth date, the 21st of June was the summer solstice and the longest day of the year. June enjoyed her birthday most of all when it fell on the last day of school which it often did. She felt that her optimism might reflect the time of year of her birth, but she knew that often she expressed cheer to try to keep those around her happy. She hated turbulence as her passionate parents often exhibited tempestuous behavior at home and she never wanted to be in the center of any kind of tornado. She knew her parents meant well, but she felt that they should contain their exuberance a bit.

June felt fortunate to have many friends. She belonged to a nice group of girlfriends, and she had two or three close friends and always had a best friend. She dated frequently so she had boyfriends, but she also had friends who happened to be boys. Since she had begun dating in junior high she had become used to dating in groups or hanging out with a bunch of friends. Many times when she met a boyfriend in the park he would have with him a few of his friends. She found it easy to make friends with his friends. The relationship felt so easy and free without romantic tension in the picture. When she became old enough to date boys who drove, her father complained about what the neighbors would think of more than one car's turning up at her house. However, her mother verbalized the theory that safety came with numbers of people together because then no solo relationship could catch fire. June knew this to be true.

At June's school the big dance of the high school life occurred in junior year with the junior prom. Here a prom queen received her crown and a lucky additional three or four girls would be named attendants. The year that June and her group belonged to the sophomore class they spent lots of time together wishing that they could receive invitations to the junior prom. However, since none of the girls in June's crowd dated boys in the junior class it appeared as though they had to miss the prom. Strangely, most of the girls in June's crowed dated either sophomores like themselves or they dated seniors. It looked as though they'd have to wait for their own junior prom. June's friend Jean decided that she and June should have a bet to see who could get invited to the junior prom first.

"Since neither one of us has a boyfriend in the Junior class, I think it's a silly bet," June said "There's such a scant possibility of our attending, bet or no bet."

"You're right, I guess. It just seems as though there must be some way."

At this time June shared a double desk in French class with a junior class boy named Glenn. She considered him a good friend, and the perfect person with whom to discuss her problems even those with boyfriends. Glenn often confided his troubles with the opposite sex to June. She felt comfortable in this relationship and looked forward to French class and the talks they had before and after class. At this time shortly before the junior prom Glenn told June that he didn't know whom to invite to the prom as he was between girlfriends at the present time. June offered suggestions mentioning girls he'd spoken of before, but Glenn seemed to reject any of the names she offered. One day shortly after the nonsense about the bet, Glenn suggested to June that she come to the Junior prom as his date.

"We'll go as friends, and it could be a real laid back date with no pressure for either one of us. I'm planning to go with a bunch of other kids. There is a party before, and another one after the prom. Would you want to go with me?"

"I'd love to go, Glenn. Thanks for thinking of it."

As Glenn had predicted even the preparations for the prom seemed like just fun minus the worry. June went shopping with Jean for a dress and accessories, and looked forward to the dance with anticipation but no fear. She and Glenn talked about it during French class, and he asked her about the color of her dress for the corsage. The junior prom itself with the parties provided as much enjoyment as she'd hoped for. She liked Glenn's friends, and the theme of the prom, Hernando's Hideaway, made for some brilliant and colorful decorating. She knew the theme came from a song from the Broadway play "Pajama

Game." Free from any romantic entanglement, June and Glenn cracked jokes and teased each other and the rest of the group they drove with. After this date June felt convinced that having friends who happened to be boys was agreeable.

Her date with Glenn had turned out so perfectly because neither she nor Glenn had tried to make it into anything more than a friendly get together. All through high school June had been involved in a friendship with a boy named Anthony. She and Anthony frequently walked home from school together, and he often complained about his parents or school problems. June also liked his closest friend, Bill, and sometimes she went with the two of them to play miniature golf. Sometimes the two boys dropped over to her house to talk sometimes arriving just as her date for the evening did. This, however, never caused any trouble for June as the just friendship aspect of her relationship with Anthony and Bill she knew to be obvious to everyone. Therefore, she showed no surprise when Anthony asked her to join him for an evening first at the movies then a walk home through the park and hot chocolate at her house afterwards.

"That sounds like fun, Anthony. Does Bill want to come along?"

"No, June, Bill has a date for Friday night."

June dressed with anticipation, but not with the usual bothersome fretting about how she'd look that evening when her date appraised her appearance. During the walk to the movie theater Anthony confided his troubles with his father to June as usual. June could stay sympathetic, as she experienced life with a strict father herself. The movie featured that evening was a comedy date movie, and they laughed all through it. Anthony frequently touched June's hand or arm for emphasis. When they exited the movie theater into the tender soft spring night, June looked forward to the stroll through the park on the way home. She readily acquiesced when Anthony suggested they sit for a while on a park bench. She reacted with shock and surprise when his hands immediately wandered over her body and his lips pressed her with a much more than friendly kiss.

"Anthony, are you crazy. This is me, your pal June. What are you doing'? Do you want to ruin a beautiful friendship."

Anthony stopped his maneuvering moves, and appeared sheepish. "I guess you're right, June. Girlfriends and dates are easy to find, but I could never find a friend as loyal and steadfast as you. You're prettier than all my other friends, too," he added with a grin..

"Do you think you're okay to continue walking to my house? Do you still want to stay for hot chocolate?"

The evening ended on an upbeat note, and June felt to her relief as though she'd handled it well. Her friendship with Anthony continued all through high school.

The last experience she had with a friend who happened to be a boy occurred when she became engaged to be married just before her birthday. Her fiancé had to be at National Guard Camp in upstate New York on June 21st", and he expressed sorrow at having to leave her alone on that special day. He arranged for his close friend, Ray, who June knew liked her and approved of her finance's engagement, to spend the summer solstice with her and help her celebrate her birthday in his place. To make the day extra special it fell on the last day June had to attend Katherine Gibbs before her graduation. June and Ray went to the movies to see Disney's "Sleeping Beauty", and ate dinner at June's house first where her mother served a birthday cake festooned with burning candies that June blew out. In keeping with most of her experiences with her boyfriends' friends, this evening proved to be special enough to apply a poultice on her missing Harry, her fiancé.

As June moved through life, she discovered that her ability to be friends with men and boys would be valuable during her career and the friendships she possessed as a member of a couple.

STARS ON THE CEILING

Jackie wondered as she rode on the bus why she felt so differently about field trips now as a sophomore in high school than she'd felt as a grade school child. She remembered that in grade school she'd been the most excited if her mother had come along as a chaperone. She'd been so proud of her mother and hadn't felt her freedom to be curtailed by her mother's presence. As a child she hadn't minded the rules-lining up, waiting, endless instructions supposedly designed for their safety. Seeing whatever museum had been offered for the trip had always seemed secondary to being out of school and away from routine. Actually, the break from routine still loomed as paramount to Jackie, and the trip represented a chance to spend a day with her friends as well as an opportunity to see something new. Jackie and the other sophomores had already visited this trip's museum, The American Museum of Natural History, located in New York City, before as children. Now, however, Jackie looked forward to what she might experience at the museum and to seeing the planetarium there which she'd never seen before. Naturally, this day no parents or chaperones marred the adventure except for teachers.

Thank goodness, Jackie thought, for the absence of her mother today as she sat with her friend Kelly on the bus tuning out the strains surrounding them about bottles of beer falling from the wall and talking about boys. Two boys in particular formed the major topic of conversation. Jackie, at the moment involved in a romantic relationship that she feared might be waning, worried about the boy concerned - Steve.

"Kelly, I think Steve's losing interest. Nothing definite has happened, but I just feel his wandering."

"You might be imagining. At least you're dating Steve. I don't even know whether Alex knows that I'm alive."

Jackie knew that Kelly had developed a major crush on Alex, a boy who won impressive scholastic awards but still held the title of comedian. She thought that Kelly had these same two attributes to go along with her red-gold hair and blue eyes. Alex, although not conventionally good-looking, exuded such an air of confidence and humor that Jackie realized that most people neglected to note that he didn't resemble Atlas. Jackie wished she could ignite a relationship between these two. Steve and Alex belonged to the same group of boys so Jackie had hinted to Steve about Kelly's feelings towards Alex, and she believed that Steve had passed the word along. Knowing Kelly's shyness, she kept neglecting to inform Kelly about this and it remained a secret.

Jackie's musings aloud with Kelly kept her absorbed for the entire trip, and soon the bus pulled up in front of the museum. Her favorite part of the museum contained the dinosaurs, and to her delight the class headed there first following the tour guide.

"I like the dinosaurs, but since we've never been to the planetarium, that's what I'm looking forward to. I understand you sit in the dark, and the stars come out over your head," said Kelly.

"That's not until the end of the day. I'm looking forward to it too. But right now do you see Steve and Alex? They're together."

"Well, in that case, I sure hope Steve pays a lot of attention to you today and draws Alex along with him."

To Jackie's delight, Steve kept glancing in her direction and flirted with her a bit as they stood in front of the dinosaur bones. This seemed to present a chance for Alex to crack some jokes about the bones, and Jackie observed Kelly's beaming. Jackie hoped that she'd noticed a small spark ignite between the two of them, but soon neglected to notice because of her concentration on Steve. During the look at the Native American and the animal exhibits, the boys stayed within flirting range without actually joining the girls. At lunch in the museum's cafeteria, Jackie registered that the boys sat at a table directly in back of them. The boys appeared to be pretending to ignore them. This constituted a setback, but Jackie had a funny feeling and said,

"I have a premonition that something astounding is going to happen this afternoon."

"If you're right, I hope it's something great," replied Kelly.

After some more touring of the museum, Jackie, Kelly and the rest of the class meandered toward the planetarium which turned out to look like a small dim theater. It gave off a cozy air, had seats like those in a movie theater and featured a black ceiling overhead. As Jackie stood with Kelly in the back of the room trying to decide where they should sit, Steve grabbed her elbow and guided her to a seat at the rear of the theater. She looked toward Kelly, and to her delight found that Alex had his hand in Kelly's as he steered her into a seat in the same row. What an unexpected happening! Music poured through the room along with the deep voice of the narrator. The room became completely dark, and stars twinkled on the ceiling. The stars over her head sparkled, and Jackie imagined her eyes sparkled too as she felt Steve's arm steal around her shoulder.

As she learned about the secrets of the universe, Jackie pondered as to how they couldn't be more mysterious than the forces at work here. She believed the auspicious stars must have arranged a day for her and Kelly even better than one they could have fashioned for themselves. Jackie knew she'd never forget the stars on the ceiling.

THE HOUSE WHERE

DICKENS LIVED

April's thoughts of London always focused first on the poets and writers who'd resided there. She loved literature and belonged to classical book groups and wrote stories and poems herself. London brought forth images of Chaucer, George Eliot, the Bronte sisters, and of course, Dickens. April planned to visit as many sites honoring her literary idols as she could while in London. April chose their hotel because it was situated in the Bloomsbury district where Virginia Wolff and the Bloomsbury group of writers lived and where they received their name. April knew her husband, Jeff, wanted to visit the British Museum and the Tower of London, and that they both wanted to see most of the other museums. On their first full day in London they took a double-decker bus tour which included Buckingham Palace and Westminster Abbey. Jeff clicked his camera constantly during the changing of the guards in front of the palace. To April the guards looked awesome in their dignity which seemed to be put on with the uniform the way little girls don a new personality when they dress in their mothers' clothes.

At Westminster Abbey April thrilled as they stood in front of Poet's Corner which contained monuments to the British literary and artistic giants from Chaucer to Sir Lawrence Oliver. Henry Wadsworth Longfellow represented the only American literary icon. After seeing the tour sites including Big Ben April lobbied for starting the museum visits by beginning with the National Portrait Gallery so that she could gaze at the Bronte sisters, Shakespeare, and Virginia Woolf. The Bronte sisters' portrait painted by their brother, Branwell, showed the three famous sisters together, Charlotte, Emily and Anne. Shakespeare sported one gold earring in his portrait. The National Gallery contained a feast of paintings from Gothic to Van Gogh. In the British Museum April ran over pointing to the Rosetta Stone when she spotted it. A crowd of tourists surrounded it, and she felt surprised to have noticed it at all.

On the second day April talked Jeff into their walking over to see Dickens's house located at 48 Doughty Street in Bloomsbury not too far from their hotel They had walked only a block or two before April expressed a fear she'd been experiencing.

"Jeff, do you hear footsteps in back of us?" They seem to start when we walk and stop when we do."

"I don't hear anything, but I'll keep my ears peeled."

After having alerted Jeff, April felt stupid. However she continued to hear the footsteps and when she looked around she saw no one. When they turned the next corner she quickly glanced back and saw the figure of a woman with a long gray braid walking in back of them.

"Jeff, there's a woman in back of us and she looks familiar."

"Well, she's entitled to walk in the same direction that we do."

April felt that the strange part seemed to be that although she heard the footsteps the entire time they walked, she could see the woman only once in a while when she turned around. Jeff surmised aloud that she probably went into the shops frequently, and he refused to worry about it any more. When they arrived at Dickens's house April turned once more, and the woman apparently had disappeared. April felt so excited to be here. She studied all the information posted in the house and read a booklet that she purchased before they commenced touring the house. She learned that Dickens finished PICKWICK PAPERS and wrote OLIVER TWIST while residing here. She went on to read that sadly, soon after he moved in to the Doughty street house with his wife and his seventeen year old sister-in-law, Mary Hogarth, Mary died suddenly of heart failure. She died in Dickens's arms. Dickens, who had been devoted to the girl, apparently never completely recovered from the shock of her death. He felt this pain more strongly than any he'd ever experienced before. The booklet continued by saying that Dickens worked this loss into his fiction, and Mary became an ideal model of femininity to Dickens, and he used this model for some of his heroines especially Little Nell in THE OLD CURIOSITY SHOP and Rose Maylie in OLIVER TWIST.

After absorbing this romantic and melancholy story, April and Jeff wandered about the house which contained treasures of Dickensiana including manuscripts of his, pens and inkwells, personal objects and reconstructed interiors. An almost ghostly mood permeated the house, and April's spirits. Downstairs in the house April felt awed as she looked at actual manuscripts Dickens had written in his handwriting. As they started up the creaky steps to the second floor April heard someone moving about. The floor moaned. However when they arrived on the second floor April spotted no one. After they perused the bedrooms including one that had a deathbed picture of Dickens on the wall, April glimpsed someone starting down the stairs. To her amazement, the person descending the stairs was the woman with the braid although she hadn't seen her enter the building. Now April was spooked, and she questioned Jeff about the incident.

"I don't know how she got up there when she did. She must have wings on her feet. Let's not worry about it," he said.

After they left Dickens's house they headed toward the Turner Museum which had been recently established. The new museum, filled with Turner's paintings, delighted April, but she still found herself thinking about the woman with the braid. As she turned around after studying one of the paintings of Venice she discovered that she now faced the woman with the braid who stood directly in front of her.

"Hi" the woman said. I guess we must like the same things. We seem to frequent the same places. I'm staying at your hotel."

While Jeff grinned, April mumbled some polite remarks and refrained from looking at Jeff whose laughter she feared might burst forth. After the woman walked away April said, "No wonder she looked familiar. She's staying at our hotel."

"So much," Jeff said, "for your mystery."

During the remainder of the days allotted to them in London they went to The Tower of London taking a boat trip there, and they took a day trip to see Bath, Stonehenge, and Salisbury Cathedral. As a final literary treat they visited Stratford-Upon-Avon, Shakespeare's birthplace, and they saw Anne Hathaway's Cottage. They never saw the woman with the braid again on their travels, but April noticed her frequently in the hotel dining room and always said hello.

SHALL WE DANCE

Christine dated boys named Al. Although she never planned to date only or even mostly Al's, it usually turned out that way. During her senior year in college a football hero named Al asked her out. She accepted his invitation although he wasn't her usual type maybe because of his name or his prowess on the football field. The evening began on an inauspicious note as she and Al stumbled over their dinner talk at the restaurant.

"That touchdown you scored today in the last few seconds won the game," Christine began thinking the subject surefire.

"Let's not talk football," Al replied, but offered no alternative conversational gambit.

Christine had heard that Al had idolized her for quite a while, but his demeanor looked more sullen than amorous to her. She felt the whole date fizzling and without apology suggested that he take her back to her dorm room.

"Sure, Christine, if that's what you want. I'll get our coats."

Once in the car Christine brooded feeling as though she'd wasted a Saturday night. The fall evening felt as crisp and invigorating as their date felt flat. Al broke the silence that reigned in the car suddenly by asking, "Christine, on the way home we pass a nightclub with great music. I know you're anxious to get home, but what would you say to stopping for a dance before we head back to the campus?"

Caught unawares, Christine agreed to his strange suggestion and soon found herself inside a smoky nightclub with inviting music seeming to pour from the walls. The band knew how to spin out music, and suddenly Christine wanted to dance. She thought Al's idea brave. He certainly had guessed that he hadn't scored a touchdown on this date the way he had that afternoon. Whatever had possessed him to suggest dancing? Actually Christine loved dancing. She'd rather dance than eat. Had someone told him? Did he know that her love of dancing only applied to dancing with men who knew their way around a dance? So few men could dance well, and he played football. She got up and followed him to the dance floor curious now.

As they hit the floor the band began playing a super fast number. Suddenly Christine lit up and she and Al began to dance. He danced beautifully, and she believed that she'd never been better. How could someone who played football be so light and deft on his feet? She thought that they danced as though they'd been dancing together for years. As the music pounded and her hair flew about Christine fell in love. Al seemed as tireless as she felt, and they danced a round of fast numbers without losing their breath. By the time the band switched over to a slow dance Christine melted into his arms and she knew she'd found her dance partner. Where there had been no conversation earlier now she thought his words fit as well as their bodies did as they danced. By the close of the slow dance numbers Christine felt that she knew Al and loved what she'd learned. Now Christine hoped the evening would go on forever. It didn't seem possible that only a couple of hours earlier she'd wanted to return to the campus.

When they started back to their table for a drink Christine worried that the spell might be broken and the former awkwardness she'd felt with him at dinner would return. However, the rapport established on the dance floor held up, and she found their conversation as stimulating as a fizzy cola on a hot day. Perhaps Al felt the same way as he chose this moment to say,

"Christine, how about going dancing next Saturday night?"

She assented, but had a further moment's anxiety as they left the nightclub for the car. What if they could only communicate while dancing or about to dance? How would he behave on the ride back to the campus? Would he become as boring as he'd appeared earlier in the evening? Her fears ended up being foolish since during the drive home she felt as though she rode in Cinderella's magic coach this time with the prince beside her. The love she felt while dancing far from evaporating strengthened on the ride back to the campus. By the time he kissed her goodnight she knew that something big had begun and she couldn't wait to see how it would unfold.

Shortly thereafter when Christine announced her engagement to her family her cousin Bill asked, "Is his name Al?"

DANCING CLASS

Life during Betty Sue's fourth grade year could be called serene. She had many friends with whom she shared her world of play and school. But in October of this soon to be eventful fourth grade year something crashed into the peaceful paradise of jump rope, jacks, and ice cream pops. Something called dancing class. One recess out in the playground her friends began talking about a coed dancing class to be held every other Friday afternoon. Betty Sue watched and listened to the babble around her and learned that everyone hoped for the coveted invitation to join this dancing class.

"Jean, are you going? Did you receive an invitation? What's it all about?" Betty Sue asked.

Yes. Most of the girls in our gang got invitations. I bet you did too. Ask your mother."

Betty Sue ran home from school and bombarded her mother with questions about the dancing class. Her mother said that yes Betty Sue's invitation had arrived, but that she and Betty Sue's father felt that the custom seemed snobbish since not everyone had been invited to attend.

"Daddy and I also agree that you girls and boys are too young to be thinking of each other as anything other than friends," she added. "Why, you and your pals still play with dolls. And you should."

Betty Sue felt in a quandary as to whether or not she should wheedle to be allowed to go. On one hand she didn't know how she felt about dancing with boys. Somehow the idea both terrified and intrigued her. However on the other hand, if all her friends planned to go, she certainly wanted to join them. The fear of being left out won over her fears about the class, and she began to lobby for going. After calling the other parents about the issue, her parents decided that Betty Sue could go along to the dancing class with her classmates. Once dancing class became a reality, it seemed to loom over the horizon like a forthcoming math test. Betty Sue worried about it constantly, and the subject of dancing class comprised all the conversations in the schoolyard and at her own and her friends' houses after school. The first dancing class, scheduled to take place in two weeks, caused Betty Sue to worry aloud to her friends about what to wear. Heretofore clothes hadn't posed too much of a problem for her. All of the other girls seemed to be worrying about the same thing. Betty Sue's grandmother whipped up two dressy dresses for her on the sewing machine-pink and blue confections made of taffeta.

One day a week before the big day a handsome boy named Arthur came over to Betty Sue.

"I'm going to dance with you and with Kitty," he announced.

Betty Sue smiled at him and filed this information away to use the next time she worried about not having a partner to dance with. His words seemed too good to be true. Many such promises rang out in the playground, and Betty Sue noticed the anticipation level among her classmates rising. Until the hubbub over dancing school began Betty Sue hadn't thought too much about boys and their difference from girls. However during the tumult caused by the advent of the dancing class she began to wonder about boys, and she and her friends even began to giggle about them. The two boys she'd most frequently gazed at were a blond Nordic looking Viking of a boy named Tony and his good friend Dick who had brown hair, dancing brown eyes, and dimples in both cheeks.

After she'd dressed for the dance on the big Friday afternoon, Betty Sue peered at herself in the full-length mirror. She looked at her new bright pink dress, but she also saw her two skinned knees. Since her knees were always skinned, she didn't quite know why they now looked incongruous. Somehow her new finery along with the skinned knees symbolized the ambiguous feelings she had about this whole dancing school caper. She had no notion how to behave, and the only person she'd ever danced with so far had been her father. Fortunately, she and Jean planned to go together and now she waited fearfully for Jean's mother to blast the car horn. In the car they admired each other's dresses and chatted incessantly about the dancing class. Once there, she and Jean clustered with a bunch of their girlfriends and began to laugh in a nervous rather than amused way. The girls gathered on one side of the room, and the boys on another. Finally when Betty Sue felt the tension in the room to have peaked, an elegant and formal looking man walked to the center of the room and asked the group to take seats in the chairs against the wall all around the room.

"We are going to choose partners and learn the foxtrot. Girls remain seated. Boys get up and choose a partner."

Betty Sue realized with growing horror that she had no choice but to sit rooted in this chair against the wall until a boy chose her as a partner. What if she were the last girl remaining in her chair? What if no one chose her? She'd never understood the term wallflower before, but now the meaning of the word stunned her. The seconds that passed felt like hours. Where was Arthur now that she needed him? Had he come at all? Could he be dancing with Kitty first? Maybe he hadn't seen her? Suddenly as the number of seated girls dwindled, Betty Sue saw tall, gangly Roger heading toward her. Roger, called a nerd by her and her friends, had never looked so good nor so welcome.

Anything but to continue sitting here alone. She flashed Roger her most dazzling smile as he reached for her hand and the foxtrot lesson started. The dancing instructor went over the steps to the foxtrot in a rudimentary fashion and when he appeared to be satisfied that they could do a semblance of the dance he ended the first dance and asked that the boys and girls be seated. Betty Sue sat down gratefully hoping for the end of the whole ordeal. Two hours must have passed by now. Unfortunately, as soon as she'd caught her breath the dance instructor made another announcement.

"Boys choose partners for the next dance."

Oh no not this again. Betty Sue felt that she'd rather die than suffer the suspense again. However, before she could panic Betty Sue watched a miracle walking toward her in the form of the godlike, blond Tony. Was he really heading for her?

"Come on, Betty Sue. Let's foxtrot," Tony said smiling.

The dance passed by in a dizzy blur of happiness for Betty Sue. She no longer pondered on the whereabouts of the probably absent Arthur. Either he'd vanished or been a no show. She couldn't care less. She wished that this dance could last for the rest of the class. When the dance ended, Tony squired her back to a chair and gave her one last sizzling smile. The next time Betty Sue heard a new dance announced she felt less scared. Her new confidence proved warranted as this time the dimpled Dick approached her chair. Both boys at one dancing class. She felt overwhelmed with pleasure. She'd passed her initiation into the teenybopper world. Nothing could ever be as difficult again.

SLEEPING IN FRONT OF THE KING

Sue Anne met Alex on the first day of school after she and her family moved to Oakdale. He lived two doors down from her, and they shared the same teacher. Each year thereafter Sue Anne found herself in Alex's class-room. They often walked home together and had many friends in common as the children in their class mingled well with each other. When they first met in the third grade Sue Anne sometimes played with her classmates as a group with the boys and girls together, but by the sixth grade she and her girlfriends had begun giggling about boys and boyfriends, and friendships began to turn into puppy love. In the middle of this eventful year a small group of boys in Sue Anne's class asked the girls of their choice for a Saturday afternoon movie date. Alex invited Sue Anne. While he might not have been her heart's choice for the date, Sue Anne anticipated the date with pleasure and thought that she would enjoy being with a comfortable boy -- one who liked her more than she liked him, but one whom she considered a friend and soul mate. After that awesome occasion, any romantic aspects of their relationship seemed to Sue Anne to dissipate, but she treasured their friendship and it grew stronger. Alex, the most intelligent boy she knew, could be counted on to understand any subject Sue Anne might want to discuss.

Even after she entered the sophisticated atmosphere of junior high school, Sue Anne's friendship with Alex continued. She trusted and respected him and believed that this provided more material for a lasting relationship than romance would. One spring afternoon Sue Anne bumped into Alex in the Junior high hallway.

"Sue Anne, I have tickets to "The King and I" at the Paper Mill Playhouse. That's practically off Broadway. My brother and his date invited me to join them with my date and to bring my friend Steve and his girl too. Would you like to go with me? My brother has his license and a car."

Would she like to go? It hadn't been that long since "The King and I" had been on Broadway, and neither she nor her friends had seen it. She would have killed for this opportunity, and here Alex stood presenting it to her.

"Alex, I'd love to go with you. Thanks for asking me. When are we going?"

After learning that the big evening would take place in two weeks, Sue Anne began to shop for a theatre dress, and she spread the news among her girlfriends. All her friends showed signs of jealousy about her getting to see the musical everyone wanted to see. On the afternoon that she bought her theatre dress, a silky off-white dress with a tailored jacket trimmed with rosy pink, she promised her friend Jean that she'd tell her all about the play and wouldn't leave out any details.

"I'm sure I'll etch the play and the songs on my memory. I'll practically perform it for you."

The big Saturday night finally arrived, and Sue Anne dressed with care and anticipated an unforgettable evening. The evening turned out to be unforgettable but not in the way she had foreseen. The date began amiably enough with the group's singing songs from "The King and I" on the way to the restaurant in the car. The songs from the show had played on the radio for a couple of years, and Sue Anne couldn't wait to experience them as performed on stage. At dinner they talked about the play.

"I saw the movie as a drama on TV. It's an old movie," Alex said.

"I'm curious to see how it will work as a musical."

"I don't even know the story. Just that the production numbers are fabulous," Sue Anne said.

"It's supposed to be a true story," Steve added.

After an excited dinner, they arrived at the theater in plenty of time, and Sue Anne learned that they had orchestra seats close enough to the stage to allow their detailed observance of the actors. When the curtain opened she discovered that she'd entered another world. The sets, the songs, and the acting seemed enchanting, and Sue Anne relaxed into the play. Unfortunately, she must have relaxed too deeply for midway into the second hour she began to feel sleepy. To her horror her eyelids felt leaden. She longed to close her eyes for a second, and the thought of this caused her to momentarily lurch awake in horror as though she'd been caught sleeping at her desk in school. She tried every trick she'd ever heard of to stay awake and to avoid nodding off again. However, the lure of shutting her eyes for a second seemed almost overwhelming. She kept glancing surreptitiously at Alex to see whether he had observed her predicament.

Just before she fell asleep during the play within a play of "The Little House of Uncle Tom" she remembered her Uncle Joe's story of why her Aunt Phyllis had married him.

"I was the only boy with whom she didn't fall asleep on a date," he'd always said.

The idea of how her slumber might insult Alex allowed her to stay awake for another few minutes, but soon she drifted into sleep for real. When she woke up the actors were still performing the play devised from UNCLE TOM'S CABIN so her nap couldn't have lasted long, but she felt flushed and overwhelmed with shame. Her cheeks seemed aflame to the touch, and she wanted to know for sure that Alex stayed ignorant of her lapse. However, Alex's demeanor revealed nothing. Her heart ached each time she thought of how Alex must be feeling if he had caught her sleeping. Once the realization that she'd been asleep sunk in, it shocked her awake, and she remained so for the rest of the musical. However, she missed the stage action because of her misery, and the rest of the evening along with the end of the play blurred in her mind. Later she couldn't recall what had happened after she woke up. She also never found out whether or not Alex had watched her napping. He didn't mention the musical or her behavior to her either that evening or at any other time. Although their friendship remained intact, Alex did not invite her on a date again. Sue Anne kept her embarrassing secret to herself telling her friends that she'd loved "The King and I", while leaving out the part about her sleeping in front of the King.

BARBARA

The essence of Barbara was like a flickering candle flame on a windy night. She was such a joyous spirit, trying to carry others along on her tide of optimism. Once, although not at that time a new mother herself, she hosted a party for all the young mothers and the children on her block so that they could meet and have kindred spirits to help each other. Her lot with men over the course of her life was, with few exceptions, terrible. Her first husband died of leukemia after a long illness during which she had nursed him. He died right before Christmas, and she remembered that the worst time had been one evening when she came home cold and weary with the tree and the children's presents and almost didn't have the heart to carry them all into the house (now bereft of her husband's presence) to say nothing of setting it all up for the children. But, of course, she managed as she always did, and the children had their Christmas.

I first met Barbara in the hospital where I was scheduled to have a gall bladder operation. She was a dear friend of mutual friends, and she walked into my room bearing a smile to warm the hearts of snowmen. She announced that she was in the hospital awaiting an operation to remove her spleen, but that her blood count had to be just right, so at the present time she had been in the hospital for a month. She informed me that she had a closet in her room brimming with liquor and cheese and crackers, and that even some of the nurses joined in her cocktail hour, not to mention her rapidly changing roommates. She was so full of kindness for me and the other patients on the floor that no one would ever have guessed how serious her own condition was. She was an angel of cheer on the floor and said it was due to the fact that a friend who worked in the hospital brought her a strong cup of coffee at dawn since breakfast wasn't served until 8:00. She was to remain in the hospital for nearly a month after I had returned home. She did finally have her operation, and a long recuperation period followed when her beautiful face was swollen from the Cortisone drugs she was forced to take. She never complained, and both of us were to view that time in the hospital as the beginning of a special friendship.

Barbara had two children from her first marriage, Jeannie and Michael. Michael was a brilliant young man with, unfortunately, severe emotional problems. Jeannie was a bright, sunny spirit; exactly the kind of beautiful, individual you would expect from a mother like Barbara. Barbara had will power like steel. She hypnotized herself so that she never ate sweets at any time because she claimed to have been a chubby child. When I knew her she was as slender as a flower stem, and Jeannie said that as much as she adored Barbara, she had always wanted a big motherly type with huge bossoms. Once when coffee prices zoomed to almost $5 a pound, Barbara hypnotized herself so that she only drank tea until the price came down. Barbara had an uncontrollable weakness about only one thing - drink. Barbara was an alcoholic; unfortunately her renown will power couldn't help her when it came to liquor. She was Jekel and Hyde-like regarding her behavior when she was drinking and when she wasn't. The alcohol in some ways intensified her essence, and she was more loving and more of a crusader when she was drunk than when sober.

She had always been involved in politics, as we were at that time, and after drinking she was known to make many a midnight telephone call sometimes to the White House itself to proport her views on the current hot issue. She also made midnight telephone calls on behalf of her friends. She once called a close, mutual political ally of ours a 'horse's ass with great justification, but to my dismay, nevertheless. Once following a misguided impulse she telephoned the Senator for whom I was a Legislative Aide on a day when he had falsely chastised me. This helpful gesture almost cost me my job, but I never had the heart to tell her. She, as usual, had meant well. This particular contretemps with the Senator and me was about who should be our next governor on the general election ballot since this was just before the primary. I was fiercely attempting to stay neutral so as not to defy the Senator by publicly supporting my candidate. A political enemy of mine had caused the Senator to believe that I was handing out literature for my candidate and displaying his bumper stickers on my car. When Barbara heard this her sense of humor again took over, and that night when we went out to the car to join her and her husband for dinner my candidate's bumper stickers were plastered all over our car. How she managed that without our knowing I'll never know, but it was very Barbara.

When I met Barbara in the hospital she was married or trying to escape from a disastrous marriage to a local rather prominent realtor. They had met while he was still involved in a troubled marriage, and he subsequently divorced, and they married. A mistake almost from the first moment. Their fights were legendary, even including an incident when he locked her out one cold, wet evening; and she almost ended up with pneumonia. He hurt Jeannie severely when he wouldn't allow her to call him Dad. He claimed that he wasn't her father. I never heard good news about this marriage, and mercifully, it was over before I even became friends with her. Barbara was a close friend of two political friends of ours, Dick and Peggy, who were having problems within their own marriage. Peggy's solution to many of their arguments was to tell Dick to go over and see Barbara. It was almost as if she were throwing them together, yet when the two of them exploded like a comet she was the one who was surprised. Barbara and Dick's love, like Barbara's life, streaked across the sky like a meteor shower. When my husband and I first saw Dick and Barbara appearing together at social functions we were a little puzzled but confused as to what it signified. Since they were obviously not sneaking around, we assumed that Peggy knew, and it was a kind of friendship thing. However, it soon became apparent that this was not the case because Barbara and Dick fell so deeply in love that they didn't trouble to hide it any longer. For both it was the first relationship in their lives where each was the most important person in the other's life. They buoyed and brightened each other's days. They couldn't stop telling everyone with whom they came in contact how they felt about each other, how lucky they were, and how they never expected to have this happen to them. When the divorce was final, and they finally married, the romance just continued and even intensified. They were so passionate about each other that they tried to share their love and joy with everyone. Barbara was always inviting the lonely to all her holiday dinners as well as giving impromptu dinners just because she felt someone needed her.

Once a neighbor of Barbara's, who was a Vietnamese refugee as were her husband and children, lost her husband. This fell at the same time as my birthday, and Barbara had invited me to join her at the Summit Art Center where she was herself involved as an artist. The Summit Art Center was having a luncheon and fashion show, and my invitation was her birthday present to me. Barbara asked me whether I would mind if she brought along her recently widowed friend. I, of course, said that I wouldn't mind, but I had grave reservations because I felt that the outing might increase the new widow's grief. My instincts were wrong, and Barbara's gesture turned out to be a healthy gust of life to the young woman. We sat in the auditorium of the Summit Art Center and were each given box lunches and something to drink. While we nibbled on our lunches the fashion show was going on. Barbara's friend seemed to really enjoy the fashions, even laughing at some of the more extreme ones. After the fashion show door prizes were awarded, and Barbara won a little painting of a Spring landscape, which she promptly gave to me for my birthday present. She even tried to trade it for a cat painting, since I collected cats, but although she wasn't successful in this, I was more than delighted with the painting I had. After the fashion show we three went to Barbara's house, and Barbara's friend said that this had been her first outing and how wonderful it had been. Over coffee and cake we three were able to discuss the horror of her experience in a way we wouldn't have been able to do without the excursion of the fashion show.

Barbara had worked all her life mostly out of necessity, and she had an important position in an advertising firm in the art department. Her marriage to Dick came about at a time when most of us were going back to work - delighted to get away from the house and child raising at last. Barbara, no longer under the financial necessity of working, happily resigned her job, and she commenced painting full-time laughing to us especially on Sunday nights,

"Tomorrow morning when I'm sipping my second cup of coffee and contemplating what I'm going to paint today you'll all be driving to work."

Staying home, painting, and cooking for Dick seemed to make Barbara happier than she'd ever been. Hers was the place I'd go to on my way home from work on a disappointing day, and though I would arrive frustrated and worn, I was revitalized by the time I was ready to leave. Barbara loved holidays, events, and parties. She threw herself into the Bicentennial with a feverish intensity - sewing all the costumes herself for the float our Party entered in the Fourth of July parade.

She threw parties and invited assorted friends from her various paths of life churned them together and waited to see what would happen. She was an irrepressible matchmaker. No sooner would a friend or acquaintance become widowed or divorced than Barbara would find him or her a match, and she would throw a party. Sometimes the matchmaking parties resulted in some rather strange pairings - two people intended by Barbara for different people would unexpectedly wind up together. When Barbara invited a newly divorced girlfriend with a peppy sense of humor who called her ex the Plaintiff, to meet a nice friend of hers, newly widowed who had a yacht at the New Jersey shore, this young woman fell instantly and hard for a disc jockey friend of Dick's who was a hard-drinking, driven and bitten man with more than one former wife. His last wife had fallen down a steep flight of steps and died. When these two met chemistry took over, and the following explosion resulted in a long affair. Although they eventually broke up, I always felt the affair had been good for both of them. He would dedicate songs to her in the early morning hours when the rest of the world was asleep and she never got over the thrill of this. Barbara was to fret and worry over this relationship the entire time it was in progress. Barbara could never understand why this sweet young woman hadn't fallen for the quiet widower she had chosen for her.

Barbara and Dick owned a yacht, and boating was their greatest pleasure. They took Mondays and Fridays off all summer so that they could have four day weekends at the boat. They belonged to a yacht club on the New Jersey shore, and they docked their boat there. Each weekend they would join the other yacht club members for a weekly Saturday night dinner dance preceded by a pre-dinner cocktail party on someone's yacht and an after-dinner dance cocktail party on someone else's boat. This was a hard drinking crew, but they held their liquor well, and they were a generally well-meaning and friendly crowd. Barbara and Dick would frequently have friends to the boat for the weekend. Barbara arranged for my husband and me to take some other couple's three children for the weekend so that they could spend the weekend with Barbara and Dick on their boat. In return it was arranged that this couple would watch our son a few weeks later so that we too could spend a weekend on the yacht.

When we did finally get to go, we enjoyed the weekend although the events seemed a bit strange to me. There were so many cocktails before dinner that we were starved and a bit blotto before we got to have dinner. After dinner there was a dance, and these people, full of booze as they may have been, were able to dance harder and longer than any people I have ever seen. Between the drinking and the dancing, we slept beautifully on the deck of the yacht with the breeze off the water caressing us. The next morning Dick took us all for a sail, and sooner than we would have liked the weekend was over. They took scrupulous care of the boat, and the time spent there and the friends they met at the yacht club were a very important part of their lives. These people made up a large part of the guest list at their parties, and we got to know many of them. I could never keep up with their drinking ability, but they were an amiable bunch.

Barbara was a special friend of the town's most ardent political couple. The woman was affectionately thought of as Pearl Mesta because she hosted many political parties, one in particular around her pool which came to be called the Sip 'N Dip. She and her husband, who looked like Ernest Hemingway in his later bearded years donated gobs of money to the party, and they collected political memorabilia. She could be quite a formidable enemy, as I had learned the many times our political paths had crossed. Once she asked me whether I would like to come and work as a secretary for her husband, who operated a small part-time business in and over the garage. I was heavily involved with politics at the time, so I refused, but did, however, manage to obtain the services of a recently divorced girlfriend of mine who needed a part-time job desperately to supplement her child support payments, which were sparse. Jennifer, the divorced mother, at first enjoyed working there and found him to be the kindest of bosses. However, before her job time there was over, she became involved sexually with him. She then proceeded to blackmail him with threats of telling his wife about their relationship unless he gave her $3,000. He did so, and she quit. I told Barbara about this escapade and about how I had warned Jennifer to be careful with his wife as she could ruin Jennifer if she wanted to. Barbara found the whole affair hilarious and called Martin, the gentleman's name, `Dirty Marty", and then she volunteered to take the job herself, saying confidently,

"He's known me politically too long to try anything with me."

Barbara was right, and she did enjoy the job, although she and Dick were beginning to tire of politics and life in our suburban town. They were tired of the friendships breaking up every spring when new political sides were drawn. They felt closer ties to their friends at the yacht club, and Dick was soon to be retired so they decided to move to the shore area to be closer to their boat and their boating friends. This move devastated me, but I tried to understand how they felt, and I knew that they were burned out politically, as my husband had long ago burned out politically; and I was nearing the breaking point myself. Strangely, when people who are involved in politics heavily do quit they tend to quit totally and don't even attend the social functions. With the exception of a life-long interest in the elections of the country and their own state, political burn out is a pretty final break with a whole way of life for most of the people who were that involved. Barbara and Dick chose a house that was at the very beginning of the shore area, and therefore close enough to their yacht club activities, but it was also close enough for my husband and me to visit as often as we could wish. I was at that time weaning myself away from a political life by working for a lawyer. Since I was his real estate secretary, Dick and Barbara used my firm for their house closing; and I was handling the paper work. About a month before they were scheduled to move, Barbara went into the hospital to have what she thought was a cyst removed. She was extremely apprehensive, almost fatalistic, about going into the hospital again. We all tried to reassure her with stories of how everyone who had had this operation was doing fine, but she refused to be comforted.

A couple of days following the operation Harry and I went to the hospital as soon as we were allowed to see Barbara. Dick took us out into the hall and told us that the doctors had discovered that Barbara was riddled with cancer, and there was nothing that could be done. We asked whether Barbara had been told, and he answered that she knew. This was a macabre explanation for the horrible backaches that Barbara had been experiencing for a year. She'd been to many doctors, and even to a chiropractor, but no one could tell her why she was suffering so.

Often when we were at her house after dinner, even during parties, Barbara would sit down and cry. It hurt her so. The next few weeks were pretty horrible. We visited Barbara as often as possible when she was in the hospital, but after she got home when I called to ask about visiting her, she replied that she was so weak that she thought she was going to die. She didn't want visitors.

Just at that time our vacation time arrived, and we were on our way to San Francisco for a week - the first time there for both of us, and we were looking forward to it. We hated leaving Barbara, but she was planning to go into the hospital again for a transfusion, which the doctors felt might help with her weakness. We returned on a Saturday late, and on Sunday Harry and I were planning to go to the hospital to see Barbara and give her a stuffed seal we got her in San Francisco because she loved seals. At the last minute I told Harry I was too tired from the trip to go, and could he go without me and tell Barbara I'd see her the next evening during visiting hours. He did go and gave her the seal, but I never did get to see Barbara the following evening. The next night as we were having dinner preparatory to going to the hospital Dick called and said that Barbara had died while he was with her at the dinner hour quite suddenly from a blood clot to the brain.

The shock waves that spread from her death were unbelievable. The next evening we went over to Dick's with some food, and all of us, including Barbara's children, broke down and cried helplessly. The funeral had so many people. Barbara attracted friends effortlessly, and she had political allies as well, so even our Congressman came looking lost and bewildered for a change.

Barbara's candle, however, has not gone out. The flickering flame of her goodness and caring shines in my heart and in the hearts of all who knew her. Her madcap sense of humor and most of all her love remain with us.

LETTERS FROM
CAMP DRUM

Each time Hank went to National Guard summer training at Camp Drum in Watertown, NY, something momentous happened for Francoise. The first time they parted for the two weeks Hank not only returned home with an elegant silver heart necklace for her but also invited her to meet his family for the first time. Nervous at the prospect of meeting so many strangers, she dressed with care wearing blue as "Seventeen" had suggested when meeting a boyfriend's parents. She took a train to the city where he lived, and Hank met her flanked by his whole family. This meeting constituted a formal change in their relationship, and the following week Hank pinned Francoise. Even if none of these life-changing events had occurred, Francoise would have been delighted simply having him home. When Hank was away at Camp Drum he wrote her a letter a day and waiting for the mailman while anticipating his letter caused the two weeks of his absence to fly as though weightless.

When Hank returned from his second trip to Camp Drum he suggested that they elope and get married as soon as possible. No one but his friend Ray knew about the proposal not even Francoise's close friend Marie. Francoise knew that Hank's desire to run away instead of planning a big wedding spun forth because they both dreaded her imminent departure for college in the fall. Hank, who had just graduated from college, told Francoise that he felt ready for marriage. This posed a dilemma for Francoise because she wanted a career perhaps teaching. She hit upon a compromise and opted to attend Katherine Gibbs as her father had always told her that Gibbs girls could get a job even when jobs might be scarce. She knew she'd get to college someday on her own. On a wonderful weekend the following March while she was attending Katherine Gibbs, Francoise and Hank got married in a small but perfect ceremony with Ray as Best Man and Marie as Maid of Honor. Francoise's girlfriends at Katherine Gibbs not only threw her a shower the day before her wedding but did her homework for her so that she and Hank could enjoy a honeymoon in Manhattan before she had to return to school on Monday morning. The letters from Hank that had arrived when he'd been contemplating their elopement again had filled Francoise with joy and intensified her romantic feelings.

By the time Hank went away to Camp Drum for the third time Marie and Ray had married and Ray had joined the National Guard too. Since Hank and Ray would be absent during the same two weeks, Francoise and Marie lived together -- one week at Francoisce apartment, the last at Marie's. This time Hank's letters caused trouble. As usual one arrived each day for Francoise while Marie received letters from Ray infrequently if at all. The situation put a strain on the girls' long standing friendship. Francoise knew that Marie must be jealous and felt a bit uncomfortable. During the second week the boys remained away at Camp Drum Marie suggested dieting so each could lose weight for Hank's and Ray's return. Unfortunately, the stringent diet caused bad tempers for both of them. The night Hank telephoned Francoise at Marie's apartment where they were staying that week Marie exploded. While Francoise talked softly to Hank Marie tugged at her sleeve and asked to speak with Ray.

"Honey, tell Marie that I don't know where Ray is at the moment."

Francoise turned away from the telephone and said to Marie, "Hank doesn't have any idea about Ray's whereabouts."

As soon as the words left Francoise's mouth, Marie must have lost it. She charged the chair in which Francoise sat and struck her cheek with her open palm.

"Marie, my God, what's your problem?"

However, since the problem seemed so obvious to Francoise she dropped it immediately and decided that a slap in the face was small payment for all those glorious letters from Camp Drum.

ALEXANDER'S BASEMENT

Molly walked home from school with Lynn that spring afternoon, and she later remembered the smell of the lilacs wafting around them. She felt tense with the feeling of danger that seemed to always surround Lynn. Molly liked Lynn, but sometimes worried about what adventure she might conjure up if she should get bored. Since at the moment three of the most popular boys in the school kept circling around the two of them with their bicycles, Lynn looked anything but bored. The boys flirted with both of them, but Molly thought that had she been alone they might have shouted a hello and then ridden on.

"Girls, here we are at my house," Alexander yelled. Let's go down to the recreation room and have a party. Just the five of us."

"Are your parents home?" Molly asked knowing that she sounded a bit fretful.

"I think so. Does it matter?"

"Sure it matters," Molly said.

"Molly, you know it sounds like fun. A party for just the five of us. I could chaperone you, and you could chaperone me," Lynn said.

As soon as Lynn registered her opinion, the other two boys-Tony and Dick, the two boys Molly worshiped most of all the boys in he school-began clamoring in a duet pleas for the girls presence.

Seeming to know that Molly presented the only obstacle to the plan, Dick called out, "Come on, Molly. Maybe Alexander's mother is home. And, even if she isn't, we're all friends. You can trust us."

"Molly," Tony added in a gentle tone, "we'd never take any kind of advantage of you. You believe me don't you? You and I have been in the same class for years."

Listening to this barrage from the other four, Molly felt worn down. She pushed aside words her little inner voice might be throwing at her and reluctantly capitulated saying, "All right, everyone, but just for fifteen minutes."

As they entered his house Alexander called out, "Mom, are you home?"

Hearing no answer Molly, Lynn and the boys trooped through following Alexander down to the recreation room. The paneled room that featured a bar and a milk shake bar in addition to comfortable looking furniture looked welcoming, and Molly attempted to relax. Alexander got cokes for the five of them from the small basement refrigerator underneath the bar, and Molly thought it really did seem just like a party. One like Lynn had thrown just a week ago that included this group and the larger group of their friends both boys and girls. No sooner had she thought this, than Dick who behaved in the boldest fashion at all times said, "At Lynn's party we played Spin the Bottle. Let's play Post Office now."

Although what Dick said was true-they did play kissing games at Lynn's party-Molly felt a growing sense of unease. Her conscience pricked, and she wondered why. Weren't kissing games kissing games no matter what the circumstances?

"Let's," sang out Lynn the flirt.

Molly said nothing as Dick grabbed Lynn's hand and led her to a walk-in closet located at the back of the room. For a few seconds silence seemed to reverberate around the remaining three louder than a gong. After what Molly deemed an eternity she heard giggles coming from within the depths of the closet, and Lynn emerged with Dick looking the same as before but minus her lipstick. When Tony took Molly's hand in hers and led her to the closet Molly's limbs shook with fear. She still felt puzzled about her unexplained terror. Inside the closet Tony kissed her softly, and told her to relax. She quietly left the closet holding Tony's hand and feeling slightly less queasy. Next Tony chose Lynn, and when they returned Alexander said, "Hey, it's my turn. Molly please come with me."

As she walked toward the closet with Alexander Molly felt less scared as she knew that Alexander harbored a crush toward her and she guessed that he would never hurt her. Once in the closet Alexander planted a quick kiss on her lips and shyly took her hand as they exited. Alexander didn't ask to play post office with Lynn, but Dick insisted on taking Molly to the closet. Molly looked at her watch and said that the fifteen minutes were up, but Dick continued his persuasion, and as Molly's crush on him ran deep, she eased herself off the couch and followed him to the closet. Once inside, Molly found her vague fears founded as Dick grabbed her and French kissed her. Gasping with shock Molly pulled away and raced out of the closet and up the stairs aiming for the front door. She never even stopped to turn around and see whether Lynn followed.

No one stopped her. Soon she discovered herself outside heading toward home and once again smelling the lilacs. Something within her had changed, however, and she could almost hear the taunts that Dick would hurl at her on his bike teasing her about the hot time in Alexander's basement. She had read about a loss of wonder and innocence but never understood what the writers meant by it. Now, she felt that in the space of fifteen minutes she had jumped from twelve to twenty without savoring the leap.

TIM DISCARDS HIS TOYS

Tim sat on the floor of his room forming plans of attack for the tin soldiers that he placed in the desired arrangement for their battle. He never tired of playing war with these obedient players on the battlefield. He spent his energy on his pretend wars and blotted out the real battlefield his home had become while his parents' divorce procedures played themselves out in front of his uncomprehending eyes. He often saw fear in his sister's eyes that echoed his own, but they never discussed what had frightened them. Sometimes Janet might say, "If Daddy leaves will we still have a Daddy? Will we ever see him?"

Tim never had any answers for her. He thought that as the older of the two, Janet should know the answers. That she didn't seemed to upset him almost as much as the questions. Although he sat alone playing in his room, he felt in the company of friends with his soldiers. Surrounding him on the shelves and even on his bed sat his cars, trucks, and planes, Tarzan and other favorite books, and arranged on a table at one end of the room his train set sat.

His toys represented a security blanket. With his toys he created a world he could control. Here he could rule or just watch the developments his imagination had set in motion. When he tired of war and didn't want to play with his cars and trucks or even the trains he could lie on his bed and reread one of his Tarzan books and enter the jungle with his hero.

"Tim," called Janet. "Let's go to the park. Mother wants to be alone."

Although this sounded ominous, Tim grabbed his jacket and a rubber ball and joined Janet. As usual as they walked toward the park they talked about trivial matters, and Tim never even asked Janet why their mother had wanted to be alone.

"Mother gave us money for an ice cream pop when the truck comes," Janet said and looked as if she expected Tim to act delighted. They returned home an hour or so later and Tim noticed nothing amiss in the house as his mother greeted them pleasantly enough. However he squirmed with unease when he entered his room. Thinking that watching his trains go around the track might help, he turned the switch. However, the familiar sounds and sights brought to life with the flick of the switch failed to work the usual magic. He turned instead to Tarzan, but his mind wandered too much to concentrate on the words. He rose from the bed and left the room returning in a few minutes with several cartons and plastic bags. He strode the length of his room contemplating and grabbed one of the plastic bags. He began tossing his stuffed animals inside the bag and then twisted the bag closed with a bag tie. Then he methodically dismantled his train set placing, the track parts and the train cars into a carton. For the next hour he traversed the room grabbing toys and stuffing them into the garbage bags or putting them in the cartons. When he'd completed the task he stood and surveyed the now stark room. It no longer looked like his room. Even Tarzan and his other childhood books had disappeared into a carton. Only his schoolbooks and some adult novels remained.

Now he grabbed the heaviest carton and started outside heading for the garbage pails at the rear of the house. Janet spied his progress as he left via the back door turning toward the garbage pails. "Tim, what on earth are you doing?"

"None of your business. I'm throwing away my toys- They're mine to throw away if I want."

"Why? You better stop. Maybe you should save them and ask Mother."

Tim ignored her words and measured his steps back to his room to grab another carton or garbage bag. Looking puzzled and bemused, Janet followed him without speaking. Tim continued his purging of his toys taking about half an hour to accomplish the task. As he worked he expected Janet to run to their mother and squeal about his actions, but she refrained from saying or doing anything at all except watch him with an expression of awe on her face. When Tim finished throwing away all the toys he'd packed he returned to his room. Janet left him alone with his thoughts as though she knew that he wished this.

As Tim glanced around his room he felt an odd kind of satisfaction. He sat on his bed and contemplated the loss of his toys. He'd expected to feel as though he'd suffered the loss of a part of his body. Instead he thought to himself that he'd passed a milestone and entered another phase of life. In some major way he'd left childhood behind him, and now he faced his grown up self free from its comfortable encumbrances.

THE GYPSY
FORTUNETELLER

Caroline wouldn't have minded so much if the incident hadn't happened on their honeymoon. On the last day of their honeymoon Kevin dragged her to an expensive nightclub located in their hometown that reportedly belonged to Dorothy and Dick, of former Breakfast with Dorothy and Dick fame. Caroline's reluctance to go that evening occurred because having just returned from the Manhattan hotel where they'd spent the previous honeymoon week, and because Monday morning back to work loomed she wanted eight hours of sleep.

"Sleep can wait," Kevin said. "This nightclub just opened, and it's expensive. We'll feel less guilty about it if we go tonight."

"OK, but if we have a rotten time, I'll throw it up to you," Caroline said smiling.

The nightclub was held on the Penthouse floor of a high rise building in the expensive section of East Orange. "You could get a nosebleed just getting up here," quipped Caroline to an enthusiastic looking Kevin. When they exited the elevator and entered the posh nightclub the first sight greeting Caroline's eyes turned out to be a Gypsy Fortuneteller. "Let's get our fortunes told or our palms read," suggested Kevin. "What a terrific way to end our honeymoon."

"All right," Caroline agreed, but as the Fortuneteller possessed long silky black hair with eyes to match, she felt a bit sulky. The Fortuneteller flirted with Kevin as she grabbed his palm and stroked it before turning it over to read it.

"My you have sexy hands," she crooned before falling silent to apparently ponder the secrets written on his palm. "You are going to have two great loves in your life."

Kevin smiled in response to his fortune, but Caroline felt like Mary Poppins when she sniffed. Two loves! A horrible thought to blight their honeymoon. She demurred when the Gypsy Fortuneteller grabbed for her own hand. One fortune told by this witch must be enough. Caroline feared learning her own. Although she knew better, she couldn't help speculating about the Fortuneteller's words. Did this mean she'd die and Kevin would remarry? Or worse yet, divorce?

"Let's go home, Kevin," she said.

"We just got here, Caroline. Let's at least have a drink."

Caroline felt that the worst part of this doomed evening must be that Kevin seemed to enjoy his fortune. He didn't appear to notice her agony. Then, too, if she shared her troubled thoughts with him he'd be bound to laugh as he didn't own a drop of superstition. She abruptly decided to hide her feelings from Kevin and get through this evening somehow. Her bad vibes about this nightclub increased when they got to the bar and perched themselves on high stools. One of Caroline's girlfriend's mothers sat to Caroline's left flirting with a handsome, elderly man whom Caroline assumed must be her girlfriend's father. When Mrs. Hilliard spotted Caroline she turned three shades of red going from pink to rose to scarlet and said, "Hi, Caroline, Mr. Hilliard's sick, and this is his brother, Bob."

Caroline assessed the situation and smiled inwardly with derision. The lie seemed so transparent and unnecessary since she didn't remember having ever met Mr. Hilliard, and if her girlfriend's mother had just kept silent, she would have suspected nothing. So far the place boasted of a Gypsy Fortuneteller and seemed to be a place that hosted at least one sleazy assignation. The evening limped on until finally Caroline, dragging Kevin by the hand, exited the nightclub and sped for home and bed. Unfortunately, the Fortuneteller's words remained with Caroline and haunted her long after she assumed Kevin had forgotten them. The one time she did bring the subject up to Kevin he laughed as she'd feared he would and replied, "Yes, my two loves are you and Nefer, the cat."

Caroline sometimes brooded over it and worried that she'd die young and Kevin would remarry. If this were the case, with whom would Kevin spend eternity? Caroline and Kevin had dreamed and planned of being little old people holding hands, walking through the park, and helping each other through the super market aisles. When Caroline hit 59 and Kevin 63 she wondered if they qualified as little old people yet. She may have been 59 on the outside, but inside she felt 18 the age she'd entered matrimony with Kevin. She and Kevin had one child, a son whom they both adored, and Caroline hoped that maybe Bill qualified as the second love.

It took a tragedy to finally settle the problem for Caroline. One summer evening she, Kevin and Bill drove toward home after dinner at Bill's favorite Japanese restaurant. While stopped for a light their Honda was hit from the rear by an RV causing the instant death of their precious son and severe head injuries for Kevin. When Kevin finally returned home to stay in time for Thanksgiving Caroline thought she might have solved the mystery surrounding the Fortuneteller's words. Kevin, due to the brain injuries, lived largely in the past remembering their honeymoon better than he remembered what he'd eaten for breakfast. Caroline had a gestalt and feared that Kevin might turn to her and wonder what happened to the eighteen year-old girl he married. She knew she looked good for 59, but 59 would look different to Kevin than the 18 he remembered. She didn't have long to wait. A week or two after he arrived home Kevin turned to her and said, "I love you. You are beautiful, but you're my second wife. My first wife's called Caroline Lee Taylor and she's a teenager. May I call her?"

Caroline looked at Kevin with a fond, bemused smile and proceeded to unearth their photo album to show Kevin the young Caroline Lee Taylor, the middle aged

Caroline, and finally the current Caroline. She also pointed out how he, Kevin, had also leaped from a slim, lithe soldier in uniform to his current handsome, but plumper self. She felt that just maybe the competition she'd spent her whole married life fretting about might be her own eighteen year old self. She felt pleased, relieved, and delighted with Kevin who seemed to be growing more like himself each day.

BALLET & TAP

Now that Jenny attended grammar school and had skipped from first to second grade, she wanted to join dancing school and learn ballet and tap. Ballerinas lived romantic lives. Jenny thought. Certainly their lives looked enchanting in the movies and in books she'd read, although Jenny knew they worked hard perfecting their art. Many of Jenny's friends had already enrolled in dancing school, and using this as fodder Jenny pleaded with her parents. They agreed readily enough, and today Jenny found herself heading toward the dancing class after school. The dancing school, located only two blocks from her house, allowed for walking there by herself.

As soon as she entered the room where the girls would practice and hopefully someday rehearse for a recital she knew she'd unlocked a magical door and what she saw inside riveted her to the spot. A ballet barre of gleaming bronze ran all along a mirrored wall. Even the word barre, Jenny knew to be French for bar, The dramatic, attractive dance instructor called the girls to attention.

"Sit in a circle on the floor," she commanded in a lightly French-accented voice.

Jenny immediately sat and watched the other girls obey too. She thought that all the girls seemed as much in awe of the instructor as she felt herself to be.

"For those of you who are here for the first time, when we enter we change into our leotards. Put your ballet slippers on first and carry your tap shoes with you. We'll work at the barre first."

As she changed into her leotard she noticed that the leotard her grandmother had made for her to dance in looked different from the leotards the other girls wore. She asked Amy. a friend from grade school, about it.

I bought my leotard from the ballet school. So did the other girls. Where did you get yours?"

"My grandmother made it. She must have copied the official one. I know my mother bought my ballet slippers and tap shoes here at the school."

Now Jenny felt a subtle difference separating her from the rest of the class, and she didn't know why this nagged at her. No one else mentioned the discrepancy in her costume, and she tried to dismiss her uneasy premonition of something's being wrong. Soon she immersed herself into the exciting lesson unfolding in front of her. First the class learned the five ballet positions. Then Jenny actually got to work at the barre. As she conquered her first exercises she knew how much she wanted to be here. She realized that her desire to learn ballet and tap hadn't been frivolous nor would it be fleeting. When they switched to their tap shoes disappointment flooded through Jenny, but she soon realized that tap could provide the lighter moments in her dancing day. She knew tap would never be her passion, but she drifted with the movements and used them for unwinding as tap came at the end of the lesson, and she learned that this would be the routine for subsequent lessons.

Jenny anticipated her future ballet and tap lessons with pleasure. Wednesday, the day of her dancing class, soon became her favorite day of the week. In between classes she practiced what she'd learned at the last lesson. She willingly worked hard hoping to achieve her first goal of being in the dance recital that, according to her glamorous instructor, would be held at an auditorium in a neighboring town. She talked incessantly about ballet and tap dancing to everyone she knew and in response to a request did a tap dance at her best friend's birthday party. She felt silly tapping among the balloons and leftover pieces of birthday cake and wished that she'd chosen to do ballet instead since she liked it best, but space didn't allow for the ballet movements. So she gamely tapped away wondering whether any of her friends could even see her feet as they still sat at the table while she danced in front of her chair.

"Yea, hooray," shouted her best friend, Annette, when Jenny finished her tapping.

Jenny appreciated her loyalty and vowed to herself to really wow her friends and family when the hoped for recital took place. She determined to work hard enough to secure a place In the recital for sure. She noticed tension surrounding the upcoming recital among the girls in the class. She knew that each girl longed for a place in the recital. The instructor talked about the recital constantly as though she hoped that holding it in front of the girls like a Jackpot prize might spur them on to greater prowess in their dancing. Jenny needed no incentive to labor on perfecting her movements. She'd caught ballet fever. Finally the fatal Friday of the announcement listing the girls who could participate in the recital arrived. When Jenny heard her name she rejoiced.

"I'm sending the dancers in the recital home with an order form to buy the ballet costume needed for the dance number. Please bring it back with you for our next class," the instructor said.

Jenny fairly flew home with her news and the order form. Her mother seemed pleased with Jenny's success but displeased about the costume.

"I'll go to your next class with you and see whether Grandma can copy the costume. She'd use a better quality of tulle and satin," her mother said.

Her mother's words filled Jenny with trepidation, but she couldn't place the source of her fear. However, the following Wednesday when she and her mother got to the dancing school, her mother tangled with the instructor who forbade the copying of the official costume.

"No official costume, no recital. Each girl must look exactly like the other girls. To do otherwise would spoil the recital."

Since Jenny knew that the money for the costume could not be a factor, she assumed that her mother would relent and order the costume. However, her mother appeared to choose to be stubborn about the issue. That evening her mother managed to get her father and her grandmother on her side in this dispute. Suddenly, her family seemed to see their honor on trial here. Jenny thought that everyone had forgotten about her and her love for ballet. Her family showed so much anger about this that Jenny knew that now her lessons might be in jeopardy. As it turned out her lessons ceased after her mother had learned that Jenny wouldn't be allowed to dance without out the advertised costume.

Jenny's disappointment over the loss of her ballet and tap lessons and the recital hit her like a shower of stones. She'd been looking forward to the time when she could wear toe shoes. The instructor had said that they had to be much older before their feet would be developed enough to permit the wearing of the toe shoes. Jenny compensated for this loss by using her allowance to buy ballet instruction books and novels about ballerinas. She even started a ballet class at her house for girls who knew nothing about ballet, had never taken lessons and wanted to learn. Ballet remained both a fascination and a mystery for Jenny since she'd missed entering its inner doors.

MARYANN MEETS PETE

Every summer Maryann's family retreated to their summer place at the New Jersey shore. Maryann had a great affinity for the ocean and the sand, but she had ambivalent feelings about vacationing there. If she met teens to hang out with the vacation almost always was great, but if none were to be found the vacation might be bleak. The first afternoon this summer on the beach Maryann spotted a tall, blond, handsome, tanned Apollo and thinking herself too shy to manage to meet him she started to pine away. This year the family had brought Lola their live-in maid to the shore with them. Lola tuned into Maryann's mood instantly and ferreted the truth from her with dispatch. Lola appeared to enjoy Maryann's amorous adventures, and Maryann knew that this year's potential romance seemed no different to her from the rest.

"Maryann, I have a plan. Just follow me. I'll do it all. You can even hide in the background. It's dark out now. Did you spy on him long enough to discover his house"

"Yes, it's one block over and one block down. I watched him head for home and followed him discreetly."

"Good girl. Let's go."

Maryann felt wary about following Lola, and she didn't trust Lola to be subtle. Still, her curiosity regarding what Lola might do or say kept her following a short distance behind her. However, she remained careful about staying in the shadows and behind bushes and trees whenever possible. Maryann thought herself to be rather daring and to have a flip sense of humor. In fact, she knew her friends believed her to be more sarcastic than she felt herself to be, and she knew they thought her to be tough. Tough she tried to be but sometimes it seemed like whistling in the dark. Maryann believed that whistling when afraid actually helped overcome whatever fear may have been lurking around. Also Lola's daring titillated her. When they reached the young Apollo's house Lola boldly strode over and rang the bell. Fortunately, the hunk answered the door himself and looked surprised to see Lola.

"Hey, Handsome," Lola crooned. "I know a little girl who'd like to bury you in the sand."

The boy looked intrigued. "Who is she'?" he asked. "Is she here with you?"

"She's hiding here somewhere. Wait, I'll find her."

"Why is she hiding" Is she ugly?"

This taunt forced Maryann out of hiding and into the light. She knew that her looks added up all the way to attractive with her sleek black hair and her unusual tawny eyes. She loved that her eyes looked like two tiger-eyes-sherry colored with yellow shooting through them. Also after having worked on her figure in years past, she knew

79

that she looked fine in a bikini. She ambled over to this tall god in shorts and smiled up at him.

"Now do you think I'm ugly?"

"No, indeed," he almost stammered.

It delighted Maryann to realize that he seemed fascinated both with her looks and with the verve she and Lola had displayed in meeting him. She took advantage of his momentary confusion to say, "Hi, My name is Mary-ann. What's yours."

"Pete," he replied. "Would you like to go for a walk on the boardwalk and maybe get a coke or something?"

"Why not?" Maryann said.

"Does, she want to come with us?" he said pointing to Lola.

"No, thank you anyhow. I have more important games to play See you sometime on the beach or the boardwalk. Bye for now."

"She's something else. Is she a friend of yours?"

"Yes, and she's also our live-in maid. She always comes up with fine ideas for adventures. She gets all the credit for this jaunt."

They strolled over to the boardwalk and played some games of chance. Failing at this, Pete tried to win Maryann a stuffed animal and succeeded in winning her an adorable Koala bear. Maryann suggested riding the roller coaster only to smile when she heard Pete reply, "They terrify me. Let's not and say we did."

Since there seemed to be no point in Maryann's going on the ride alone-indeed it might seem like showing off she agreed to give the ride a skip and suggested the

Ferris Wheel. He acquiesced to this plan, and the two boarded the Ferris Wheel. From the lofty vantage point at the top when their car stopped there, the moon and stars appeared close up and personal. Apparently, Maryann thought, they both felt romantic at the same moment as Pete kissed Maryann just as she thought about it. After the kiss Pete seemed as pleased with himself as Maryann did with herself, and the rest of the evening rocked. They shared cotton candy and hot dogs and continued to try the games of chance with no success. Pete walked Maryann home and they arranged to meet on the beach the next morning. The next day started a pleasant routine that lasted for the rest of the two weeks both families planned to stay at the shore. Maryann and Pete sunned on the beach swimming only long enough to cool off. Maryann modeled her four different bikinis and took turns wearing them. At lunch time they shared the picnic lunch Maryann had had Lola provide. And Maryann did bury Pete in the sand.

"A promise is a promise," she teased.

The afternoons spun themselves out in the same fashion as the mornings, and it seemed a lazy, peaceful interlude the long days winding themselves out slowly like a long velvet scarf. The heat felt sensuous. The water felt crisp and blessedly free of jelly fish. Maryann loved Pete's massaging suntan lotion on her back and shoulders, and he seemed to enjoy the process almost as much as she did. They both swam well enough to be able to frolic in the waves, when the mood struck. Surprisingly, Pete seemed to enjoy reading as much as Maryann did which pleased Maryann as most of the boys she'd dated never opened a book. Reading formed a large part of their languid afternoons. Pete told Maryann that he attended Upsala College located two towns away from where she lived and that he lived in the same town and commuted to school. Maryann found this marvelous as it meant that this delightful relationship had a chance to survive the vacation. Maryann's sense of humor and daring helped her from feeling inferior due to her being four years younger than Pete's 20 years. She might have been sweet sixteen, but she'd been kissed many times. When their mutual vacation ended Maryann began to hope that he would call as soon as possible so that her torture of waiting might be as short as possible.

Once home she immediately made the mistake of telling her best friend, Sue, about Pete. Sue had a myriad of questions which Maryann reveled in answering, but now having confided her summer romance to Sue she had put herself on the spot as to Pete's telephoning her to resume the relationship. For four long days she agonized each day's holding forth less hope of his calling. She knew Sue tried to help by chirping optimistic sayings, but Maryann became close to frantic. If only she'd said nothing to Sue she could have handled Pete's apparent rejection. Finally on the fifth day after Maryann's return from the shore, Pete telephoned. He said nothing as to why he hadn't rung up before, but he did ask her out for the upcoming Saturday night. He owned a car, and this date started a whole romantic relationship. Her fears turned out to be groundless, and Sue cheered and said, "I told you so!"

Maryann enjoyed their becoming an item -- a twosome and eventually a married couple. Not a bad resolution to Lola's little prank.

FIRST FIGHT

Until It happened Mary Sue's romance with Kevin had sailed along as smoothly as a boat in calm waters. She'd anticipated today's events with pleasure looking forward to her mother's making spaghetti and meatballs for all of her friends, most of whom had never tasted genuine Italian spaghetti sauce before. To top off the dinner party, Liz who together with her boyfriend Jim made up one of the invited couples to Mary Sues' dinner party, had volunteered to host a dessert party at her house, just two or three houses away from Mary Sue's house. The dinner party started off swimmingly with the four couples clustered around Mary Sue's dining room table which today held the extra leaf to accommodate the couples gathered around it. Mary Sue's mother's spaghetti and meatballs tasted succulent as always and silence descended except for the clink of silverware tinkling on the plates as the group of couples ate. Suddenly Maryann commented, "My mother's spaghetti sauce tastes much spicier. She uses more garlic and even green peppers.

"Maryann, one fallacy that persists is that genuine Italian cooking contains oceans of spices. My mother's family's sauce lacks excess spices. The flavor of the tomatoes and meat bubbles through. Isn't this delicious?"

The remainder of the guests had mouths too full to answer. But Mary Sue watched the relish with which they ate and felt satisfied that they agreed with her. Maryann always had at least one negative comment to contribute, but Mary Sue attributed it to some mysterious jealousy that Maryann held toward Mary Sue and whatever Mary Sue had involved herself with Mary Sue noticed that Maryann's plate emptied as quickly as the other plates, and she smiled to herself as Maryann grabbed a second helping and piled the spaghetti high on the plate. After the sated guests thanked Mary Sue's mother for the sumptuous dinner, the group left in one body to walk to Liz's house in the scented spring evening.

Later Mary Sue thought that the conversation at Liz's must have set Kevin off. Kevin's, being four years older than Mary Sue, qualified as one of the oldest boys in this group of Mary Sue's close friends. Only Pete, Maryann's boyfriend and a fraternity brother of Kevin's, could be said to be on Kevin's level age wise and otherwise. Liz's Jim, was in high school while the four girls were seniors, and Betty's Fred, a Prep school boy but still only in high school. Mary Sue knew Kevin felt to be juvenile. The conversation floated in a silly but jovial way about events in high school as the senior class graduation day approached.

"Jim," Liz giggled, " Mary Sue doesn't want Kevin to know which side she's marching on in case she makes a fool of herself during the promenade."

"Absolutely, true," Mary Sue answered. "I'm so exhausted and tired of marching, to that tiresome and icky "Pomp and Circumstance.""

"Icky? Really, Mary Sue how childish," Kevin commented.

"See, it's not even graduation night, and you are casting aspersions on our rituals," Mary Sue said.

"Not on your rituals, Mary Sue, on your vocabulary," Kevin answered.

At this point Liz interrupted with a welcome diversion namely chocolate cake, and Mary Sue watched the group's attention wander from her and Kevin's fight. Not so her mind, she felt as if it were stuck in a groove like a broken record, and she wearily kept going over the things Kevin had said. He'd sounded so sarcastic and snobbish. She'd never before thought of him in those terms. Being the top actress in her high school she feigned acting oblivious to Kevin's insults and carried on joining in the party glee with jokes and anecdotes relating to the coming festivities. Everyone agreed that the continual marching in the spring heat to the strains of "Pomp and Circumstance" felt like a drag, and everyone claimed to be anxious for the ceremony to be over and for them to be duly graduated. Mary Sue's pretending carried her through the rest of the party, and she wondered what would happen once Kevin walked her home, and they found themselves alone in the T.V. room.

Soon enough here they were, and instead of their usual kissing and hugging rituals before parting a fight broke out instead. Mary Sue discovered herself crying with anger and frustration. Kevin looked puzzled by her outburst. "What on earth are you crying about?" he asked.

"You humiliated me in front of my close friends, and you ask what's the matter?"

"Mary Sue, it's just that listening to you and your friends I suddenly envisioned us at a party with my boss and business associates and your using the word icky as you did tonight. It makes me wonder whether you're mature enough to ponder marriage."

"Me, not mature. I didn't insult you in front of a bunch of your friends. Of course I'd know better than to use that word in front of your boss. When in Rome. I just happened to be in Rome tonight lest you forget. Think about it. I spoke in front of my friends in my milieu, remember? You are the outsider. You're as bad as Ed Norton's and Ralph's thinking that icky meant fat because Alice used it to insult Ralph."

Kevin looked chagrined. He started to apologize haltingly, "I'm sorry If I hurt you, Mary Sue. Maybe I'm a college snob looking down on you high school kids. If so, I apologize. Okay?"

Mary Sue needed no more. She glanced at him and when he opened his arms she melted into them. As they first embraced and then kissed she hoped that their future fights would end as painlessly as this one.

SUMMERTIME

"and the living is easy. Fish are jumping and the cotton is high" poured forth from the car radio that first summer of Suzette's marriage to Kevin. "Porgy and Bess", the movie, opened that summer, Suzette bought the record album of the musical and played it day and night in the small apartment. The musical's songs sang and echoed in her ears and her heart. One soft summer evening as the strains of "Summertime" made the car hum as Suzette and Kevin sang along, Suzette murmured, "Let's make this our song."

"Why not," Kevin agreed.

They'd married the March before, and Suzette considered this summer their official honeymoon. Since they'd only had a weekend honeymoon, her father treated her and Kevin to a trip to Washington D.C., airfare included. Although they'd returned early in the summer from Washington, Suzette thought their honeymoon just begun. She kept busy making the apartment their home. Years later when Suzette saw "Barefoot in the Park" she remembered this first apartment. They chose honey beige paint, and the paint didn't turn out quite right. The apartment consisted of two rooms, a bedroom and a large outer room for every purpose except sleeping. This room contained a living room, dining room combination and a kitchen hidden in a closet that Suzette kept closed unless she needed it for cooking. They owned a stereo; Kevin's pride since he'd built it himself with superior components, an original painting by Suzette's brother Bill, the artist; new bedroom and dining room furniture; and borrowed or donated furniture filled the other empty spaces. This un presuming apartment shouted love, however. It contained Kevin's beer mug and stirrer collections and records, Suzette's books and collected treasures. New curtains in a honey nut brown completed the room along with flower arrangements. Suzette thought her modest apartment a palace. She felt sorry for ordinary mortals who lived in proper houses.

Although they felt complete together wrapped in their love like a cashmere sweater, they invited their friends, single and married and sewed them together into a patchwork quilt. They loved giving parties, and their instincts proved right since the parties consisting of people from all the different parts of their lives took off. Kevin's stereo worked overtime at parties where the amplified strains of "The 1812 Overture" filled not only the walls of the apartment but rang out over the courtyard causing a near eviction one warm night when the music boomed forth for Suzette's guests and her neighbors. The super said the next morning, "Everyone within shooting distance of the courtyard called me to complain. Another party like that one and you're out."

When alone with Kevin, Suzette reveled in their love. Often on weekend evenings, they'd go to bed and wake up sometime before midnight. Hungry Kevin would suggest calling for pizza. Often he'd bring home roast beef from the deli especially for midnight snacks with rye bread. Since they both worked, they often dined out. Their favorite haunt featured the best pizza this side of heaven. After they'd been married for years Suzette would talk Kevin into making a pilgrimage to The Star for that pizza that never changed its recipe. On weekends they ate at the fancy restaurants in their area, and eventually had tried each one. When their routine called for friends Suzette felt they had a colorful bounty from which to choose. Suzette's best friend, Maryann, was married to Kevin's closest friend, Pete. Almost every Friday evening the foursome met and talked and laughed over pinochle. Once during an argument between the men and the women, Suzette and Maryann ran around Maryann's apartment shouting "Rape." Something that at that time Suzette found hilarious. In today's climate she knew no one would ever joke about rape. When Suzette felt like comfortable company she and Kevin joined her cousin Andy and her husband Rich for movies, rides on summer evenings, or just get-together's at each others apartments. When Suzette met a young married couple who loved to laugh named Phyllis and Bill she incorporated them into her circle of young married people, and she and Kevin, Phyllis and Bill, Maryann and Pete, and Andy and Rich all enjoyed each other's company. Life seemed rich in its textures and tastes. Their unmarried friends came to visit too. Each time she had a fight with her mother Suzette's cousin Christine would unexpectedly ring Suzette's doorbell. Often she arrived at an awkward time, and Kevin would answer the door looking like Omar the Tentmaker. Fortunately, all three could see the humor in this situation, and it created laughs at the time and for years to follow. Suzette and Christine often sat up all night talking and sharing secrets about Christine's boyfriends and their own shared past adventures. Suzette furiously made matches for Christine and all her other unmarried friends and double dates ensued. When the married couples starting having children, the children could be brought along in car seats and portable cribs. The women shared maternity clothes, baby clothes and furniture, and had play dates for their babies that doubled as gab sessions for the mothers.

In the three years before Suzette and Kevin became parents, their life spun along with enough money, clothes, and free time to splurge. Splurge they did, and their happiness infected those with whom they came in contact. If Suzette and Kevin had problems in those years, they had to do with their landlords the O'Gradys. Mrs. O'Grady constantly moved Suzette's furniture never bothering to apologize or explain why she'd found herself in their apartment in the first place. Mrs. O'Grady also eavesdropped shamelessly, and instead of being ashamed of herself she'd pass along advice based on what she heard. "Never, tell your mother anything. She'll only interfere. Young people should be left on their own." The irony of her words never hit her. Mr. O'Grady drank. Suzette wouldn't have minded, but the source of his supply came from her liquor cabinet and the cabinets of the rest of the tenants. He watered down their bottles. Once she and Kevin felt sure about this practice Kevin devised a plan. He lettered a sign saying "O'Grady keep out" and pasted it inside the hall closet over the shelf where they kept their liquor.

Within a week after Kevin placed the sign, Mr. O'Grady dropped dead of a heart attack. Since neither Suzette nor Kevin had heard of any prior heart condition they felt guilty. "Maybe," said Kevin, "he croaked when he saw the sign."

"Oh, Kevin, he couldn't have. Just coincidence."

Coincidence or existing heart condition, they never found out. Shortly after Mr. O'Grady's death Mrs. O'Grady moved away, and the mystery remained unsolved and stored in the annals of Suzette's memories. The carefree existence of those first three married years helped to sustain Suzette during many troubled or turbulent times that came later. When she became pregnant with a much wanted and anticipated child, she and Kevin moved from their nest filled with love in the city to the suburbs where she'd spent her own childhood in preparation for the birth of their son. With his birth, "Summertime" continued more than ever their song.

WITH DADDY & MOMMY STANDING BY

Surely, we did stand by as he grew from a sturdy, rosy child to a strong but gentle man, and when he felt sad, discouraged or even depressed. We wanted to be a shelter from the bullies in his world, a buffer from the teasing and taunts that we remembered as part of childhood. He took himself seriously as I tried to encourage him to laugh at himself, but he also took the feelings of others as seriously as he took his own. He stood up for and defended his friends and his loved ones. When he'd grown to manhood and started teaching his college students, he championed them and their causes too.

I tried to be sensitive to his emotional ills as well as his physical ones. Certainly, I put in my time at all night fever vigils, but I also tried to sooth his emotional turbulent seas too. Once when in grade school, homework and peer pressure had taken their toll on Bill, I intervened and sent him to Florida to visit his grandmother for a week with a bonus I'd received at work. Once again when he felt bogged down in a swamp of work and social obligations while in graduate school and adjunct teaching, I contributed tickets for my husband and me and Bill to Italy during Christmas break. Bill invited a good friend, and the vacation cheered us all.

Bill returned our caring with waves of love of his own. He actually seemed proud of his parents and looked forward to our coming to see the shows in which he appeared at college. Once when he attended graduate school at Drew University he brought me along on an afternoon visit to the campus library and bookstore, and the two of us ran into the Dean. Bill seemed to grow taller as he said looking pleased, "This is my mother." You would have thought he had just introduced his Dean to Jackie Kennedy. I remember that day with a rush of warmth because my book group had decided upon reading the first novel written, PAMELA, and I had no idea where to locate it.

"Mother, let's go to Drew. Either their library will have it or they will order it. Maybe the bookstore will have a paperback copy. Let's drive over to the campus."

He turned out to be right. The library ordered me a copy, and the bookstore did indeed have the book. I bought a copy and wrote postcards to the other members of the group advising them as to where they could obtain copies of PAMELA. Bill seemed as pleased as if he'd solved a problem of his own. He had such a generous spirit. Once when he lived and taught in New York State at a small college there I told him about an upsetting experience I'd had that morning at the Hairdresser's. During an animated discussion I'd been having with my hairdresser, the hairdresser in the booth next to ours interrupted us to say, "You are not really a happy person. You are a sad person masquerading as a cheerful person." Even over the phone lines he managed to cheer my spirits, and the next day the local florist delivered a bouquet of red carnations (my favorites) from Bill with a card saying "To make you even happier."

Bill liked to say it with flowers, but not at the expected times. Often Mother's Day might go by without a word from Bill, but the following Saturday afternoon he'd send a gorgeous and unique bouquet of say Bird of Paradise and Tiger Lily flowers. One week after mother's day he sent me red carnations, my mother-in-law pink carnations (her color of choice) and my mother yellow long -stemmed roses as she considered any other flower an affront. He didn't like occasions that he felt the business and advertising worlds promoted. He hated Santa Claus as he felt that he took all the glory of Christmas away from Christ.

He distributed love equally between his two sets of grandparents even though each set wished to be the favored ones. Once when he'd recently purchased a lime green Volkswagon he drove for two days from New York State where he lived to Florida to visit my mother. She never forgot the unexpected visit from her Grandson in his new bright green car. It really did resemble a slice of fresh lime color wise. As a college professor he demonstrated his caring for his students by expressing interest in the things they cared about, taking them on field trips to New York City for the first time, writing recommendation letters for them, and even seeing one boy through a nervous breakdown. He advised the drama club, headed the

94

honors society, and became a literacy volunteer. He never begrudged the students or the college his time. He believed himself happiest when teaching or serving his students or the college. Many of his students took all the courses he taught, even when they could have taken the same course with some other professor at a more convenient time for themselves.

Yes Daddy and Mommy stood by, but Bill stood by them and all those with whom he came in contact. Unfortunately, his life ended in a burst of brilliance in its summertime. He never reached the fall or winter of his life. But he scattered more sunshine in his short thirty-seven years than most people do in seventy. Then he spread his wings and took the sky.

WHO'S JADED NOW?

During the thick of the noise, paperwork and afternoon heat, Ruth heard Joan say to the group at large, "Aren't you thrilled about Senator John Kent's appearance tonight?"

"Thrilled about meeting another politician? Ruth countered. I'm jaded by this time. I couldn't care less."

"But he's gorgeous, and a pro football player to boot," Joan continued.

"A former pro football player. Besides they all put their pants on one leg at a time," Ruth continued her negative commentary.

After having worked in the political arena for years by this time, Ruth had met many Senators and Congressmen as well as Presidents Ford, Reagan and Bush respectively. Right now her desires could be fulfilled with a cool shower, and a gin and tonic with maybe a chaise lounge to lie back in. Golf Outing day proved as hectic as the weeks of preparation before it when Ruth had to make up foursomes from among the people accepting the Party's invitation and arrange the food and country club arrangements. She'd been here behind the reception desk at the Golf Outing since 8 a.m. after having been up till 2 a.m. the night before handling last minute preparations. Fortunately, soon they could head to the club's locker rooms to shower and change into evening clothes for the formal dinner after the day's golfing.

Joan seemed to find Ruth's attitude so amusing that she busied herself by telling all Ruth's friends and political allies what Ruth had replied to her question. For some reason the rest of the group laughed and teased Ruth intermittently for the rest of the afternoon even as she headed to the locker rooms to change.

"Ruthie, I hear I have no competition from the Senator?" quipped her friend and colleague Rob.

"My heart still belongs to you, don't fear," she shot back. "Why do you all think what I said so damn funny?"

"It's just that the Senator is considered to be quite a ladies man, Heartthrob too according to my wife."

"I repeat, Rob, I am by this time jaded."

After a cool shower and a change into a slinky, cool black dress and evening shoes, Ruth felt as refreshed as if she'd just plunged into a burbling mountain stream. Her spirits had cooled as well as her body. After her first sip of the long awaited gin and tonic she felt ready for anything. Anything perhaps but the sight of a Greek god standing slightly apart from but surrounded by a crowd of people. That must be the famous John Kent. No wonder they laughed at me. What a hunk. I'll just keep my cool and not let on that he got to me after all.

"Ruth," the County Chairman called, "Come over and meet Senator Kent, I want to take a picture of you the way you look tonight in that dress with the Senator."

Ruth cursed the excitement pouring through her as she tried to look nonchalant approaching the gorgeous political icon. "Hi, it's nice to meet you," she managed to mumble before the photographer snapped three pictures of them. She murmured a quick prayer that the snaps of the two of them would come out well enough to mount and frame. Not everyday did she get to pose with a Senator cum movie star. Her flustered state unfortunately gave her away and left her open to the teasing of the entire assembled group as to her remark about being jaded. She rued her big mouth. Why did I have to pontificate? Now I'll never hear the end of it?

Her friend Rob especially taunted her all through dinner, and when the County Chairman rose to introduce the Senator during coffee and chocolate mousse Ruth heard his words and shuddered. "The Senator is not only a distinguished political figure, but a hunk even to a jaded woman in the political tent." Ruth writhed with embarrassment as Al, her County Chairman, mocked her offhand remarks. She knew she'd never live those remarks down no matter how long she stayed active politically. Rob laughed, squeezed her hand, and his eyes twinkled with guffaws she knew he truly tried to suppress. Rob's good-night sally to Ruth became a password for her colleagues. As Rob pecked her cheek saying goodnight he smiled and asked, "Who's jaded now?"

A PRIZE FROM
MISS WALLY

Amy's first three years in grade school rolled gently by taught by sweet young women who seemed to love children. Therefore, she found Miss Wally an unpleasant discovery as she looked formidable with her perpetual frown and forbidding since she never spoke kindly to her young charges. Her face appeared set in cement, its wrinkles etched as if in the clay of time. To Miss Wally belonged the task of teaching the children fractions and the finer points of grammar. Heretofore, Amy had found that schoolwork came easily to her, and she surmised that her friends hadn't much trouble either. Fourth grade proved to be the exception-a challenge to Amy and she thought for her peers too. Miss Wally broke her habit of sternness only when dealing with the rich, clean-looking, blond children in the classroom.

When the first Friday rolled around Amy watched in horror and turned shades of green with jealousy when

Miss Wally announced, "I'm thinking of a number from 1 to 100. The child who comes closest to guessing the number wins a prize. Write down a number from 1 to 100 on a piece of paper, add your name, and pass it to the front of the room."

As Amy had feared when Miss Wally started the game. Miss Wally awarded the prize to a lovely, cameo-faced, blond girl named Rosemarie who evidently ranked high on Miss Wally's favored child list. Amy's emotions churned within her. She experienced anger mixed with the fiercest jealousy she'd ever had since her little brother entered the household. Knowing that she herself could be thought to be an ordinary looking child, slightly plumb with black, curly hair, she held out no hope for future Friday prizes. How she wanted that prize-a silver compass pointing north. As the Fridays wound on Amy watched bitterly as the favored few raked in their prizes, a brightly hued book with maps called an Atlas, colored pencil sets or boxes of crayons, drawing paper, and notebooks.

Amy mentioned the situation at school to her mother, and her mother appeared to ponder the matter for further consideration. About six weeks after the opening of the school year, Amy's mother attended the school's Open House. When she returned that evening she called Amy over and said, "Your Miss Wally and I hit it off. We discovered that we're both twins. Sit tight this week, and don't be surprised if things change for you. Be patient and wait."

Amy held out little hope for change. After all, she still didn't possess blond hair or blue eyes even if her mother and Miss Wally did chat. She expected life in the fourth grade to continue on its disagreeable way with her and her friends watching from the sidelines as the chosen few reaped their rewards for being favored with gold dust in their looks and manners. The first Friday following her mother's visit to the school Amy cringed when Miss Wally announced the game. She held aloft that week's prize-a red pencil box that Amy coveted on sight. Never had she desired one of Miss Wally's prizes more than that red box. It contained two layers holding, pencils, pens, a ruler, crayons, and a compass. She knew she'd hate the recipient of this treasure with even more heat than she'd harbored toward the past winners of the contest. She wrote down her number, placed her name at the bottom, and passed the scrap of paper towards the front of the classroom. She felt no thrill of anticipation and knew that 99% of the class felt the same. Miss Wally read the slips of paper and boomed out the news that today's prize went to Amy.

Amy's joy leaped up to the ceiling. She walked toward the teacher's desk on legs of jelly marveling that they held her up. She accepted the pencil box gratefully, and held it close to her chest all the way back to her seat. As she delved into its contents she found them as wonderful as she could have hoped. She felt that this had been her greatest day in the fourth grade. Could any other day so far rival this one? Her friends gathered around her showing jealousy but also happiness that one of their own had finally received a prize. Could Miss Wally be changing her ways and playing the contest fairly at last? Amy along with her friends hoped that would turn out to be the case, but memories of her mother's words echoed inside her head. She feared and hoped at the same time that she'd become one of the favored ones.

As the school year began spinning itself out marked off by the holidays-Halloween, Thanksgiving, and Christmas Amy's luck held. Miss Wally rocked to and fro among about five children whom she showered with the prizes taking turns so that each of these chosen children received a prize approximately every five weeks. Amy found herself in a quandary as to what she should do about this situation. As usual, she first consulted her mother whom she considered to be wise in the problems of the world of adults. "Mother, Miss Wally still plays favorites with the prizes. She cheats. Everyone knows that she does. The only difference now for me is that I'm one of the special ones. No one has said anything to me, but I feel guilty. Should I go up to Miss Wally and ask her to play fair?"

"Amy, if you confront her you'll place her on the defensive. That means you'd force her to admit what she's been doing. She'd dislike you for daring to see through her little games. I don't know what to tell you. I'll think about it."

Amy puzzled over her mother's words and figured that they made sense. She continued to ponder the problem. For a while she did nothing, but around the time of the Christmas break she received a set of reference books bound in something that looked like red leather. Amy thought about her classmates and from the group chose a studious, shy girl named Ruth whose family didn't have too much money. Amy felt that not only did Ruth deserve the prize for her schoolwork, but that the prize might add a little Christmas cheer to her holiday. She didn't wrap the gift but as soon as they went outside to the school yard at the close of the day she tapped Ruth on the shoulder and said, "Ruth, take this prize. You deserved to win it, but as

Miss Wally obviously won't play fair, let's try to fix the problem ourselves. From time to time we'll all get together and pick someone to receive the prize I get. But, let's keep it a secret from Miss Wally."

Not only did Ruth seem pleased, but when Ruth and Amy shared their plan with the rest of the class excluding the other privileged ones the class raised a cheer. They seemed glad not only for a chance at an occasional prize but at the opportunity to put one over on Miss Wally. Amy knew they all felt as she did that Miss Wally asked to be deceived. For the second semester of the school year, every once in a bit someone who'd worked hard actually earned Miss Wally's prize albeit without her knowledge. Amy went home and praised her mother for her sensible words and revealed her plan for fairness to her. Miss Wally continued practicing her bias never knowing that her prizes once in a while fell into the correct hands. Sometimes, Amy thought, justice assumes strange guises.

ABOUT THE AUTHOR

Susan C. Barto was *born* on the beautiful day of June 21, 1941. The beloved child of Eda and William Forcellon. As she grew up she met a terrific man (Harry W. Barto) who later became her loving husband. Later Susan gave birth to a handsome baby boy (William M. Barto).

Susan's *educational* background was developed at Katherine Gibbs School and Union College, NJ. She has traveled extensively to Egypt, Italy, England and France.

She has experience with two years Legal Secretary - Legislative Aide; A writer for the last ten years. Her *memberships* include President Friends of the Hunterdon Museum of Art — New Providence Library Board, NJ — Raritan Valley College Book Group.

Susan Barto's *honors* are: Golden Certificate Award, Drury's Publishing™ — Plaque from Library Board, Listed in 1999-2000 Who's Who In The East and 2000 Who's Who In America, and Who's Who In Literary Achievement.

Her *publishing credits* include eleven stories published with Creative With Words, One story published with Yesterday's Magazette, One story published with Writer's Guidelines and News, One story published with Good Old Days, and several stories published with Drury's Publishing™, along with four books of stories published by Drury's Publishing™.

On a more *personal note* Susan C. Barto says: ***"I love to write. Writing defines who I am."***

www.ingramcontent.com/pod-product-compliance
Lightning Source LLC
Chambersburg PA
CBHW050350030726
47503CB00008B/2714